*SACCULINA*

# SACCULINA

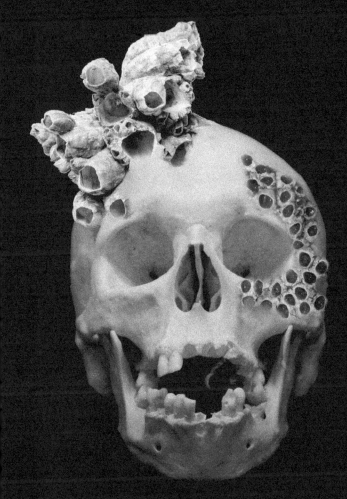

## PHILIP FRACASSI

*This one is for my dad.*

THE BOAT WAS too small.

That was Jim's first thought as he stepped from the truck. His legs broke out in goosebumps, and his eyes throbbed from lack of sleep. The two cups of gasoline station coffee made his groin ache and tingle with the need to piss. When he saw their boat way at the end of the dock, he could only think how very tiny it looked. Other boats loomed around it, white and shiny and unsinkable. Beyond them, the pink dawn was beginning to weave itself into the gray edge of the Pacific. The air was fishy, cold and damp. The soft rocking and creaking of the boats emanated from the docks and seagulls flapped their wings somewhere nearby, cries distant and wary. One of the men farted and sighed, someone else hocked and spit, as they started toward the water.

Jim followed his brother Jack across the concrete pier and onto the chipped-wood of the wide dock. He glanced down, past his shoes, through the soaked slats, to the hem of the ocean below. Even at a couple feet of depth the water looked alive; suds and trash felt up the thin shoreline like a thousand lapping tongues, each as hungry as the last. He shuddered and brought his eyes up to follow Jack's shoulder-blades, which protruded sharply from beneath his frayed Mello-Yello T-shirt, the same damned one he'd had when they were kids. But as he'd been wearing an orange jumpsuit the last six years, Jim figured he probably didn't mind, likely found the old clothes comforting. Like going back and starting over from a certain point, rewinding to when you were nineteen and still harbored thoughts of a brilliant future.

Jack wasn't that kid, not anymore. He'd grown older, harder. In the weeks since he'd been home the changes, physical and psychological, were more evident. Jim didn't like how skinny his big brother had become, for one. His face had hollows it didn't have before, and his arms were sinewy, his elbows knobby. He wore his old jeans but they hung low, even with his broad leather belt pulled to the last set of bolt holes. His hair was short now, choppy, sticking from his skull in matted black clumps.

Up ahead, their father Henry led the way. He was wearing khakis, a Polo pullover and a cheap ice-blue windbreaker. His thin graying hair played with the breeze, his shoulders slightly hunched. He was young, having just turned sixty, but life had taken a toll on him, and Jim knew he was physically old for his age. Sadness and loss did that to a man—took from him. Took from the inside out, so that by the time you saw the results it was too late to do anything about it. What was done was done. Life was a merciless thief with a black heart, and you hoped it passed you by when scouting for its next victim. Jim knew life had visited their home more than once and didn't think the old man could take another calling.

"Mind the seagull shit, little brother," Jack said as he kept pace behind their father, stuttering his stride to make sure he didn't pass him. He turned his head, gave Jim a look. His brown eyes twinkled and Jim saw the curl of his lips. He was loving this. How could he not be? Fishing with his old man, ready to cut through the waves, deeper and deeper into the blue Pacific, the salt spray on his face... Jim didn't doubt this was one of many dreams Jack played in his mind on cold nights while lying on a ratty cot, staring at the ceiling of his tiny cell out in Lancaster, the local branch of the California State Prison for those boys and girls who live in the "who gives a shit" part of the Golden State.

Bringing up the rear behind Jim, humping a full-size red metal cooler, was Jack's best friend, Chris Hanson, who looked every bit like a 280-pound kid, wearing a filthy Dodgers cap, thick plaid shirt and heavy brown cargo shorts, his wide calves emptying into loosely-tied Jordan high-tops. Chris had been Jack's best friend since they were, well, since forever. Jim couldn't think of a time when Chris wasn't around, and he'd watched the two of them get into so much trouble, time and time again, that it seemed by the time they were teenagers the old man had finally given up trying to keep them in any sort of check and focused his efforts on Jim—his last-ditch effort of raising a good son—instead of his eldest. Their mother's untimely death hadn't helped.

Jack hadn't been able to deal with the year-long horror show that was their mother's slow demise. The three surgeries all but bankrupted their father and left them all emotionally cleaned-out, their feelings of love and support so scrubbed from inside their heads, their hearts, that nothing remained at the end but cold finality. Inside the pale room at the community hospice where they'd taken her to die, Jim watched her last breath with dry eyes. His father had crumpled to the floor and lain there. While the nurses struggled to get him to his feet, Jim stood rooted to the bleached linoleum of the hospice floor.

Jack walked out.

They had been kids at the time. Jack only eighteen, a senior at East Bakersfield High, a run-down school backed up to an Amtrak station, the inconsistent running of the trains a background hum that made the classroom windows vibrate. Jim a sophomore, not even driving.

Afterwards, their father went through the motions of burying his wife, and himself with her in a way. Both boys knew he was lost to them. They could see it in his eyes. Could feel it. Love had run out of stock in the Lowell home, and only a great emptiness remained.

Jim filled that emptiness with his hobbies—his books, his computer, his game console. He was a serious gamer, and when he wasn't reading dog-eared philosophy texts or his favorite science titles—Hawking, Kaku and Sagan, may his soul rest in peace—he spent his nights writing juvenile code for games he created in his mind, then committed to paper before attempting to create the thing in one of his developer programs. After a couple years taking tech classes at the community college, he'd been confident enough to send a few of his more developed samples off to different companies, the code and the links to his lame beta levels, but none of them ever replied. He started a YouTube channel, spent countless hours reviewing games, posting video of fixes and cheats, slyly promoting his own early visions. It passed the time, got him through high school, those four dull-eyed years of being a Bakersfield College Renegade.

Got him through the loss of his mother, the emotional loss of his father, and, shortly thereafter, the loss of his only brother to a first-degree burglary charge.

Turned out Jack had been breaking into houses around the neighborhood, stealing whatever he could easily sell to a couple guys down in L.A. who moved the stuff. Laptops mainly. But any tech would do. Smartphones, tablets—those were a thief's modern-day treasure, replacing the outdated silver flatware or the proverbial pearl necklace.

When Jack was sentenced, their father fell even further into his spiraling depression. Within two years he had lost a wife and his oldest son. He tried with Jim, tried to be a father, but when Jack was sent away for six years, it broke him completely. Whatever was left of him to give sputtered and went out like a dying flame, leaving Jim to his solitude. Each of them became a ghost the other shared a house with—and quiet ghosts at that.

Now Jack was out. And maybe, Jim hoped, maybe things would begin to go right again. To make sense. To be whole. Jim wanted a family, a life that wasn't filled with heated-up dinners and silent, solitary nights. Wanted his big brother back, wanted his father to laugh again. He hoped that day would come. And hell, he thought, a guy could hope, couldn't he?

Jim and Chris had driven out to Lancaster to pick Jack up the day of his release. Jim brought Jack's old leather jacket, his favorite baseball hat and the pair of dusty black Ray-Ban's that hadn't moved from the top of his dresser in the six years he'd been gone.

Chris had stopped at a liquor store and bought a Styrofoam cooler, a bag of ice, a 12-pack of Budweiser and a fifth of Jack Daniels. "Essentials," he'd said over his shoulder, as the old man behind plexiglass rang them up.

Fully stocked with booze and memories, they waited together in a broad, empty sunbaked parking lot, the two of them staring at a twenty-foot high barbed-wire fence and the stoic, blocky red-bricked building beyond with equal amounts disdain and fear. They didn't speak. They weren't friends. They were parts of Jack, disassembled and left to wait patiently for his return.

Jim often wondered if Chris had been with his brother on those break-ins, with him on the night he was chased through a neighborhood—like the criminal he was—by angry policemen, dogs and the all-seeing spotlight of the chopper following him through yards and over fences. Jim wondered if Chris had been the lucky one that night, and he wondered if it was Chris's stupid idea in the first place.

He never broached the subject, not out of fear, although there was certainly an intimidation factor. Chris was a big guy. Six-feet and a lot of change, arms coiled and bulging, barrel-chested and topped with a shaggy mop of long brown hair, his face and neck covered with it like fungus. He had deep-set blue eyes and a famously broken nose. He worked construction with his father, so his fingers were coarse and strong, thick and bent as stubby tree branches. He never bothered Jim when they were growing up, barely ever paid him any mind at all. Didn't tease him, didn't protect him. Jim meant nothing to him. No, Chris was Jack's through-and-through. He was his shadow during their early years, a wraith that always hovered just over his smiling brother's shoulder, arms folded, waiting and impatient for whatever the two of them were going to do next, double-daring anyone to lay a finger on his skinny, jackal-eyed best buddy. And while Jack may have been the smarter of the two, Chris was more thoughtful. Where Jack was mischievous, Chris was dark, brooding, and prone to sudden violence. Jim never knew what Jack saw in him, but we don't always pick our friends, don't always choose the companions we share our lives with. And maybe, Jim wondered, it wasn't about Jack picking Chris. Perhaps it was Chris, all along, who had settled himself on Jack.

When Jack walked out from the prison that day, Jim didn't give Chris a chance to one-up him. He ran to his brother and embraced him. Jack laughed, pulled Jim away so he could look at him, smiling and crying. Jim was startled at how much older his brother looked, skinnier now, with a moustache that was too big for his thin face. But his eyes still sparkled, and his grip was strong as weeds.

"Look at you," Jack said, tears running into the teeth of his broad smile. "Little brother," he said, and they hugged again.

"I brought your jacket, and a hat," Jim said stupidly, giddily. "Dad's waiting at home."

"Yeah, I figured," Jack said, still smiling. They made

it back to the car and Chris. The two grown boys, now men with history, embraced, and Chris patted Jack heavily.

"Don't do that again, huh?" Chris said, then turned and got into the driver's seat of the old Thunderbird he'd driven since the day he turned sixteen. Jack winked at Jim, who gave his brother shotgun, and they went on home.

THEY REACHED THE end of the dock and the worn-out, depressed-looking, twenty-foot fishing boat. The words Not A Chance were written in looping cursive along its hull in shit-brown letters, faded by the sun and corroded by the salt of the sea. Jim's mouth dropped open at the site of the thing, the stern sagging, nearly level with the low, lapping waves. The rear deck, where all four of them were supposed to fit, pulling in fish and relaxing in the sun, looked as cramped and cluttered as a trailer-trash living room.

"Hope we don't sink the little fucker," Jack mumbled to Jim, giving Chris's mammoth girth an exaggerated look before he turned with a flashing smile to greet the captain, who stood on deck waiting for them, hands on hips.

The captain, who introduced himself as Captain Ron, was an old, white-bearded man with a gut that hung like a barrel. His paunchy face was a deep shade of beet-red and he wore a thin, stained, white button-down short-sleeve shirt, dark green suspenders attached to worn-out jeans with no knees, and grimy brown leather sandals on his broad, hairy feet. His wardrobe was topped by a weathered trucker's cap that read LAS VEGAS across its wide front, two rolling dice with frayed stitching falling hopelessly between the barely legible LAS and VEGAS. Jim noticed that the captain had bits of food stuck in his dense beard, and his eyeglasses were so thick that Jim could easily count the red veins in each bloodshot eyeball.

The captain stepped up to Jim's father and stuck out a meaty hand. Henry looked to Jack questioningly, as if he hadn't the damnedest idea how to respond.

Jack stepped up and clasped the captain's hand, pulled him up to the dock. The captain swayed a bit, rubbed at his forehead, and eyed each of the men respectively. "Ayuh," he said, his voice breathless and wet, "I see there's four of ya."

Jack glanced wide-eyed at Jim, just for a moment, a frantic look of are you serious, then back at the captain.

"Yes sir," he said, waving a hand at the others and talking in a condescending tone Jim figured the captain couldn't catch. "There's the four of us. That's what we discussed." Jack made introductions.

The captain sighed and waved his fat hand, as if things like life or names didn't really matter anymore. He turned his back on the men and looked at the boat, then out to the sea.

"Well," he said, sadly shaking his bowling ball of a head, "I'm sorry, lads. Not today."

The men on the dock shared quick exchanges. Chris stepped forward. "Not today what?" His deep voice rumbled like Neptune.

The captain turned, eyes bulging behind the dense lenses. He brought a finger to his red, veined nose and scratched. He looked at each of the men who stood, waiting.

"Can't," he said, as if it were the most obvious thing

in the world. He pointed to the ocean, gave Henry his full attention, adult-to-adult. "Wind's ripe wicked, sir. The waves, they're rough. We'll toss like salad out there. Not safe, not really. Not great for fishing, that's for sure."

Henry turned toward the younger men, his thin fleshy face hanging from his skull, his eyes wide and curious. "He says weather's no good," as if they weren't all standing a foot away when the captain had spoken.

Jim bowed his head, groaned, and rubbed his eyes. This was so typical for them that he really wasn't surprised. And he was tired, so very tired.

They had driven into the hotel parking lot a little after nine p.m. the previous night. Driven three hours from Bakersfield to the marina, booked two rooms at a crappy hotel near the coast. But the Kings were in the playoffs. Game six had taken a total of five and-a-half periods to decide the outcome. Nearly three overtimes, with intermissions, had kept all of them up late, glued to the room's tiny television, pulling on their quickly-depleting case of beers and cheering their team on. By the fifth period, Jim was fighting to keep his eyes open, Henry was snoring in an ugly lounge chair, but Jack and Chris were pulled right up to the screen, sitting side-by-side in cheap wooden table chairs, punching each other and howling with each near-score, drunkenly laughing. The room lights had long been turned off so that only the television's one-eyed glow illuminated their mad, grinning faces.

They roared and high-fived when the Kings finally put one in, waking Jim from his awkward place on the floor and making Henry beg them (for the hundredth time) to go watch it in the other room.

From half-lidded eyes, Jim studied his brother, his poor, thin older brother; noticed how his face reflected the blues and whites from the television, his skin pale but his eyes wide and shining with life, with freedom.

He groaned and crawled up onto his bed fully-clothed, hardly noticed when the two men slapped his ankles as they walked from the room, talking loud enough to wake the entire floor of the hotel. Jim smiled, happy that the Kings scored one for his brother, glad they were able to share the moment. Even if he was asleep on the floor when it happened, they had still been together.

But Jim was feeling less gracious a mere three hours later, when the alarm went off at five a.m., waking them for their charter. Henry was up like a shot, making coffee, already dressed by the time Jim was able to roll out of bed, his head haunted with beer dreams and the dull throb from lack of sleep.

"Morning, son," his father said, handing him a coffee. There was a banging at the door, happy voices in the hall.

It was time to go.

And here they were, after the drive, and the crappy hotel, and the late night. They had actually made it to the dock, miraculously, on time. Made it down to the shitty boat, ready to fish the deep blue waters of the ocean for god-knew-what. And now this fat, sloppy, cartoonish captain, with his long white hair and bushy beard, his thick glasses and his Las Vegas trucker cap, was telling them the weather's too rough? The waves too high?

Jim shook his head. "Bullshit," he said, loudly enough that everyone looked at him, Henry in shock, Jack with a half-smile. Jim stepped past them, right up to the captain.

"We chartered the boat to go fishing, man," he said. "Unless there's a hurricane coming, or you've had a Jaws sighting, we're getting in that boat and we're going to go out there," he pointed to the ocean for effect, "and fish."

The captain, even more wide-eyed than before, looked to Henry, then to Jack, who simply shrugged.

"Look," Jack said, calmly and with good humor, "if it's a danger thing, we get that. But if it's just a matter of it not being ideal weather, we'd like to give it a go. My anxious little brother here is a little worried because, well, he really loves to fish."

Jim had never fished before in his life. None of them had as far as he knew. But when they asked Jack what he wanted to do, what would be the most fun "out of jail" event they could throw together, he immediately suggested a fishing trip with the men. Not that there were any women to speak of, but Chris warmed quickly to the idea, and who was Jim to complain? Their father called around, found a charter, and scheduled a day. It was easy. They didn't need to provide poles, or bait, or the boat. It was all part of the deal. Part of the package. It was an expensive package, no doubt, but Henry found a way. Jim thought Henry, in his quiet way, was actually pretty excited about the idea.

Maybe he could make it back, Jim thought while watching Henry talk through the trip itinerary with Jack and Chris over pizza that first night of Jack's freedom. Maybe he could get back to being the father he once was, the man he once was. If not all the way, then part of the way. Enough to add some years to his sad life, to let him wake up a little happier in the morning. Enough to make him their father again.

"Not to mention he had a few beers last night... well, this morning," Jack continued, smiling openly at his little brother. "So, look, if it's a matter of rough water, or poor fishing, we don't really give a shit. We just want to get out there, into the water and, you know, have a nice time."

The captain rubbed a hand over his mouth, looked at Jack, then Jim, then turned and looked at the water. He walked to the edge of the deck, spit over the edge, watched whatever happened to his saliva when it hit the churning water below. He glanced at the sky, the lightening cloudbanks, the oncoming yellow glow of God's morning piss melting through the slate-gray sky.

He turned, rubbed his chin. "Alright. I think we can go. But if it gets too choppy, yeah, we gotta come in. My call," he said, tugging at one suspender. "Captain's call."

Jack clapped his hands together and Jim let go of a breath he didn't know he'd been holding. Chris let out a "fuck yeah" and climbed heavily into the boat, causing it to tilt wildly before he found the middle, balancing it out. Henry followed, then Jack hopped in right behind him.

Jim went to follow, but the captain put an iron-firm hand on his shoulder. He turned Jim toward him, stared into his eyes. Jim swallowed, suddenly terrified of this large, bristly old man. He smelled tuna fish and cigarette smoke on the captain's breath, could count the coarse black hairs protruding from his nostrils. The captain leaned in close, his firm hand tightening.

"You look weak to me, yeah? First time on a boat, yeah?" He smiled a little, his wet lips curling deep within the nest of white hair. "Well, when you gotta puke, boy," he said, in an almost inaudible whisper, "and you will have to puke... you do it over the side, ya hear? Not on my boat. And not in the head, see? Over the side. I ain't working a mop, ya get me, kid?"

Jim nodded. "Whatever, man, I got it."

The hand squeezed once more, then released. "Good," he said, smiling wickedly. "Then in you go, sonny. We've fish to catch!"

The captain bounded into the boat, and Jim, still stuck to the dock, turned back without reason, looked once more toward land. He saw their father's brown truck, alone and dark in the parking lot off the pier.

Beyond the rim of the hollowed-out buildings, he could see the sun rising in the east, pink and swollen and wrathful, urging him onward, promising him that, ready or not, the new day was coming.

He turned away and stepped into the boat.

THE FUMES FROM the engine were already making Jim sick, and he wondered if it was a good idea after all to brave the whipping wind and wild waves of the angry sea.

Chris and Jack had cracked open the cooler and were holding cans of Budweiser, their eyes glued to the sprays of water and the broad expanse of ocean beyond as the boat cut through the waves, engine roaring like an angry demon, white smoke trailing from behind them. With every rise and crashing fall as the boat crested wave after wave after wave, Jim was sure the stupid thing would crack open like an egg and spit them all into the frigid water. He shuddered at the cold and at the small stab of unease that buoyed in his guts at the thought of being pushed into the dark sea, swallowed a bubble of bile that came up into his throat. Carefully, he leaned toward the cooler, tossed open the lid, pulled a beer from inside—purposely ignoring the clear plastic bags of sandwiches, frosted with moisture from the processed meat that lay within. He slammed the cooler shut, sat back onto the rigid bench, waited for the boat to crest a rather nasty wave, then cracked the beer and drank. The cold bitter liquid soothed his throat, washed away the unease, cleared his aching head.

Better, he thought. Much better.

He looked across the boat, saw his father watching him. Jim nodded, motioned with the beer as to offer one to his old man, but Henry just gave a small smile, his sad eyes twitching away, back toward the sea.

Thirty minutes later, just when Jim thought he would be forced to jump over the side to escape the teeth-grinding, mind-numbing whine of the motor, the thick, gagging fumes of gasoline, and the constant rise and fall of the boat as they smashed their way into the ocean's broad belly, the engine abruptly quieted and the boat slowed down.

The captain let the boat idle, making the fumes and exhaust even worse than before, no longer whipped away behind them, but now settling over the deck like a pungent, poisonous gray cloud.

"Well, okay, it's rough, yeah," he barked from the open standing shelter that housed him. "So, here's the deal, it's too rough to fish where I'd like, too rough for you boys, for sure. So, okay, there's a piece of real estate about another, oh, hour or so out."

Jack and Chris shared a quick, wary glance. Another hour? Jim swallowed, lifted his shirt over his mouth and nose, tried not to think about his stomach.

"Yeah, about an hour," he continued, as if they'd asked the question out loud. "But, but... it's deep. Real deep. More than six thousand meters if you can believe it. Cold and dark and still, well, more still than this. Lots of fish. Albacore, Yellowtail, maybe even Barracuda. That'd be a story for your friends, eh? So, that's my plan. Any objections?"

They all looked at each other, stupid and sleepy and sea-sick. No one spoke. "Right," the captain said, pulling off his grimy cap to finger his bald pate, scratch at the long white hairs surrounding his wide dome like an encroaching serpent army, "that'll be that, then. On we go."

Henry spoke up. His wobbly voice timid in the thrashing air, his frame tiny against the wide blue carpet of sea surrounding them. "Captain Ron," he said, trying to sound authoritative, at least. "Is it safe?"

The captain turned, looked at Henry, then toward the coast no longer visible to the naked eye.

"Safe?" he said, and chuckled, a raspy, dark, clunky thing that left his mouth like the exhaust fumes from his vessel's engine.

He eyed each of the men, a small smile on his fat, doughy face. His googly eyes settled on Jim a moment, then flicked around to the others before turning his broad belly back toward the controls.

"Ocean ain't never safe, Mr. Lowell," he said over his shoulder, gunning the engine. "Thought you boys knew that!"

CHRIS WAS THE first to get a bite.

After a grueling hour Jim would not soon forget, the boat settled in the area the captain had sold them on. Once the engine cut and the fumes cleared, Jim agreed the water did seem calmer than what they had cut through during the last hour. It was a rich, heavy blue, and if he looked down at it long enough, he thought he could make out the black void in lie beneath their relatively microscopic vessel, the deep cold water resting just outside the sun's reach.

The boat rocked steadily, the wind strong but not the twisting gusts it had been. The captain set up eight fishing poles, each pointed to the sky in its own iron sheath, the hooks baited, the lines taut as they reached for prey. He'd given two poles for each of them to watch, under instruction to call him over when there was a bite.

Despite the fresh salt air and the lack of fumes from the extinguished motor, Jim had already vomited over the side of the vessel—twice—and his face felt waxy and blood-drained, his throat raw, his stomach tight and pruned. Jack and Chris had laughed, of course, but Jack handed him a fresh beer each time, something to "get the stink off his tongue." Their father looked a little green himself, but somehow managed, at least up until now, to keep his seasickness contained.

At least now they could settle themselves and finally begin to enjoy the excursion. They kicked back and watched their designated poles.

They'd been lounging no more than half an hour when the sun made its presence known, the heat causing them to shed their outermost layers, flannels and jackets tossed in a pile atop a box of old rope and stained life vests.

The sudden jerking of the pole, followed immediately by the whinny of the reel being pulled, brought them alert, and even Jim, sick and miserable as he was, popped to his feet at the sudden adrenaline rush of the moment. Chris all but leapt at the rod, grasping it in two hands and lifting it deftly from the holder, a giant, nervous smile breaking over his face.

"Whoa! I got one," he yelled.

"Let 'er run a bit," the captain said from the wheelhouse, watching the distant ocean as if he could see the fighting fish dancing in the dark cold depths. "Give it line, there's plenty there. Let's get her tired, yeah?"

Chris, flushed with excitement—the buzz of the six or so beers only a whisper in his head now, drowned out by the frantic, inherent screams of the hunter—pulled back on the rod, the reel spinning and whining in his hands. He stood, knuckles white, muscles of his bulging arms flexing as he waited for the moment when he could fight back.

"What do you think it is? Feels strong as hell," he said over his shoulder to the approaching captain.

"Yuh, it's got some speed to her, that's for sure. Could be anything, there are sunfish that could pull a man clean off a boat, a' course that's more down south a ways..."

"Should I, you know, reel it in?" he asked.

The captain looked to the reel, slowing now, then back to the sea. He nodded. "Yuh okay, real slow, though. Let's see what kind of fighter we got here."

Chris began to turn the reel, inch-by-inch he brought the line back in, each rotation causing the reel to click in response. The rod was bent over like a thin black rainbow, the exposed line shimmering with seawater in the morning sun.

"Woo! Yeah!" Jack whooped from behind Chris, all of them watching the pinprick where the line entered the ocean body twenty yards distant. "Bring that little shit in here, big guy."

"It's really fightin' me," Chris said through clenched teeth, the reel clicking slowly as he turned it, bringing the catch closer. "It must be a big sucker."

The captain put a hand on Chris's shoulder, gently, his eyes never leaving the water. "Easy now," he said softly, reassuringly. "Take 'er slow." He reached down to the side of the boat and picked a long net off two rubber yellow hooks. He held it up vertically like a wizard's staff, then extended it over the back of the boat. He reached out with his other hand, gently curled a finger around the taut fishing line.

"Should hold," he said, but without much confidence. "Don't know what you got there... but it's an angry S.O.B., for sure."

They all waited, Chris groaning but obviously exhilarated, the rest of them keeping one eye on his victim, the other on their own poles, making sure they didn't go taut with a similar catch. They were expectant, a little afraid, unsure of themselves in the strange environment, so far from familiar things. What did they know of fishing? What did they know, these kids from the dusty streets outside Bakersfield, of the great ocean?

Despite the sport and the adrenaline of the moment, Jim couldn't shake the sudden feeling that they were surrounded, in a menacing way he could not comprehend, by endless water and unknown creatures. In his mind, the boat was nothing more than a dark blob floating in the bright blue sky of the ocean's underworld, unaware of all that lie beneath, blind to anything that may lay waiting under the surface of this alien landscape, biding its time before striking. A boat like theirs could easily be toppled by a rogue wave, the passengers tossed into the sea, food for the elegant monsters below. In the deep water, they could be killed even by the curious; against intent they'd have no chance at all.

Chris was sweating now, his arms shaking, his feet shuffling. Jack stepped to his side, leaned over the edge of the boat.

"You want me to take it, just for a bit? Let you rest?"

"Hell no!" Chris said, so loudly it seemed blasphemous in the blue cathedral of sea and sky. "Ain't no way I'm letting some fuckin' fish get the best of me, man, no way no how."

"All right, all right..." Jack said soothingly, smiling. He glanced at the captain, who shrugged, as if saying, you asked for it, here it is. Good luck.

Minutes passed, and Chris kept turning the reel, and then, finally, about ten yards out, something broke the surface.

"What the hell is it?" Chris asked.

"I... well, I dunno," the captain said, sounding uncertain, confused. "Looks like a sea bass, and not a very big one, but I'll be damned if it ain't fighting like a shark."

He poised the net over the water, feet spread apart, braced. "Keep 'er coming now…"

Suddenly, in a flash of slick gray and a burst of spray, the fish leapt from the water, no more than ten feet out, wriggling in the air as if it were being electrocuted. It crashed back down, vanished.

"Holy shit!" Jim yelled, a stupid smile plastered across his face. "Did you see that thing?"

He punched Jack in the shoulder and the brothers smiled at each other, just two little boys again, in awe of something wondrous.

"What's wrong with it?" Henry asked.

Henry stood timidly to the side, stiff and unaffected. His eyes were fixed on the broken water where the fish had slipped below the surface and out of sight.

The captain turned on Henry, annoyed.

"What's wrong with it is it's pissed off!" he said, and gave that dry chuckle again. Jack laughed as well, buzzed on Budweiser, loving the freedom and thrill of the moment.

"No, I mean, I know…" Henry said, embarrassed. "But it doesn't look right."

"Well," the captain replied, "it's gonna look like dinner if the big man here can get 'er in the boat."

Jim studied his father, who shrugged and continued staring at the sea. His disconnection to current events was palpable, the emotionless of him in sharp contrast to everyone else on the boat, a shadow in the bright sun.

"There she is!" the captain yelled, and Jim leaned forward, could see the thing wiggling in the water, just a few feet away now. It was big, but not huge, and he couldn't help feeling let down the by averageness of the fish. It was maybe a foot-and-a-half, a streaking, snaking thing. "Just hold 'er there..."

The captain dipped the net into the water, brought it up from underneath the fish, surrounded it. He angled the pole upward, lifting the netted fish high into the air, its fight now diminished to twitches and the occasional flop, spraying them all with its oily wet residue. Jim studied it as the captain moved the net back into the boat.

Henry was right, he thought. It did look strange. It looked very strange.

It was longer than he'd thought, now that he could see it closely, maybe two feet, and thick, like a child's thigh. But the skin was wrong. It was... lumpy. There were black, pinecone-sized knobs on it. A bunch of them.

The captain whistled. "It's a nice fish, although the liberals frown on keeping the sea bass, but I ain't gonna say nothing. Here, get the hook outta there while I hold it. You!" he barked, his eyes on Jim. "Open my fish hatch, right there." The captain nodded his head at a handle in the boat floor, and Jim, without time to be pissed for being ordered around by the fat bastard, bent over the handle and hauled it upward, revealing a mildewed basin below.

Chris was finishing with the hook, but frowning as he worked, disgust on his face. "What's that on him?"

The captain held the netted fish over the deck, let it hover over the waiting hatch. He looked at the fighting, desperate creature, squinting at the black knuckle-shaped protrusions that dotted its head and side. Jim counted at least five of the things.

"I'll be damned," the captain said, moving as close as he dared, the fish's glass eye staring back at him. "If I didn't know better, I'd say those are barnacles."

He tapped a finger through the netting, poking one of the hard crustaceans near the fish's head that all but covered one of its wide, black eyes. "Ain't that something," he mumbled, then slowly lowered the fish, still tangled within the large net, into the hatch. He flipped the rod and the fish dropped out of the net and onto the plastic bottom of the hold. It flopped madly, dying slowly from lack of water-fueled oxygen, suffocating on air. The barnacles stuck to the fish scratched the white plastic, scraping savagely as the fish twisted and wrestled out its life.

"I have never seen anything like that before," the captain said quietly. "No siree. That's a new one."

"What? I don't get it," Jack said, stepping forward to look at the bass, all of them now in a tight circle around the hold. "Is it uncommon or something?"

"That's one word to use. Bizarre might be another," the captain said, setting down the net. "We should take some pictures of it, maybe sell it off to some nature magazines, newspapers. I've been ocean fishing for forty-some years, yeah? Ain't seen nothing like this."

"What's so strange about it?" Jim asked, studying the fish, now lying still, its stomach rising and falling quickly. "Barnacles aren't uncommon, are they? Aren't they always on boats and stuff?"

"Yeah, they are," the captain said from his knees, staring intently at the crustaceans stuck to the fish's skin. "They're also on whales, sea turtles, big fish like that. They cement themselves, see, to the fish, to the skin. Then they let the fish take them to the food, the plankton, whatever. Crabbers like to find 'em, as it means the crab ain't shed recently, meat's better, richer. But I'll be damned, I sure ain't never seen one on a sea bass. Doesn't make sense."

"Why not?" Henry asked, bent over despite himself, all of them talking quietly, as if they were studying a sick child, or a dangerous, trapped beast.

"See, this ain't a whale, Mr. Lowell. This is a bass. It's way too small for a barnacle, they wouldn't waste their time on such a creature."

He bent down, grabbed the fish tightly in one hand, then, with his free hand, gripped one of the black crustaceans. He pulled, groaning slightly, and Jim could hear the sick, squelchy ripping of the bass's flesh as he yanked the barnacle free. Blood spurted from the spot it had stuck itself, quickening the fish's death, reddening the hold.

The captain held the barnacle up for them all to see. "This is an unusual little guy." He turned it over. "See the bottom here, where it's got all the fish skin? That's where it laid its cement, its glue. On whales, for instance, over time the skin of the fish will be ingested, up into the barnacle, to increase the strength of its hold. And this opening here..." he flipped the thing over, revealing an eye-shaped slit at its top, "that's where it feeds. It's a parasite, I guess you could say. Or, at the least, a freeloader."

He chuckled once, but his heart didn't seem to be in it. "This one's awful big," he continued, "and I ain't never seen one on a fish like this. Never."

Chris reached down and gently pulled the barnacle

from the captain's fingers, studied it closely.

He poked the opening and tiny tentacles—they looked more like skinny white earth worms, Jim thought—swarmed around the tip of his finger, latched tight. To his credit, Chris didn't scream, or panic, but simply raised his arm and showed them all, one-by-one, as if the thing stuck to his finger were his favorite baseball card and this nothing more than elementary school show-n-tell.

"Dude, that is gross," Jim said.

The captain stood, slowly, and studied the thing attached to Chris's finger. "It's trying to eat you, son," he said.

With the slightest of frowns, Chris flicked his hand sharply, and the black thing shot away. They all watched it fly through the air, back toward the mysterious deep, where it plunked into a rolling wave, and disappeared.

THREE MORE HOURS passed and they caught no more fish. Not a bite. Not a tug, not a nibble. Nothing.

And then there was the bubble.

They heard it first. Or, more accurately, felt it.

A rumble of sorts. The kind of low, vibrating sound you'd get from a subwoofer. They all froze, glanced nervously at each other, at the boat, at the water.

No more than fifty meters away, the waves went flat and there was a rippling in the water. A circle in the sea, the breadth of a football field, took shape.

As they watched in fascination, the mammoth disc of restless water rose into several broad, sphere-like, but translucent, bubbles.

"What the hell?" Jack said, but no one answered.

The bubbles rose, some ten meters high at their peak, the bright sunshine glimmering along their surfaces in an oily rainbow dance.

And then, one-by-one, they silently popped.

The ocean returned to normal, the waves picked up, and a massive gust of sulfur swept over the boat, making Jim gag and hold a shirt over his mouth and nose again until the breeze carried it away.

"Well, I'll shit," the captain said, and went back to his controls.

"Maybe an underwater volcano," Henry offered, and took a bite from his sandwich.

Jim felt too sick to care, too hot and bored to offer his own version of the event, and as nothing else of note occurred as the hours went by, they forgot and focused on staring at the mute fishing poles, the dead lines, and thinking of the useless, floating bait sunk below.

Eventually, Jack and Chris slowed down on the beers, full and sleepy and tired of pissing into the sea. Jim had one bite of a ham sandwich, felt his stomach gurgle unpleasantly, and opened a bag of chips he had stowed in his pack. Henry put on a wide-brimmed hat, sat quietly eating his own lunch, legs up on the bench as if he were on a veranda instead of a small, swaying, stinking fishing boat.

The captain kept fussing, getting more and more anxious about the lack of fish, but refusing to come right out and apologize or offer any solutions. He checked his gear, stared at his Doppler, drank a beer, helped himself to a sandwich, pissed off the front of the boat and belched and sighed as they all baked in the heat.

The ocean, at least, had calmed. Jim thanked the gods for that, because if the rocking had kept up he would have puked up the four beers he'd already drank since they'd settled into this calmer spot of sea. The thought gave him a disgusted craving for the quickly-depleting stash floating like dead mermen in the now-sloshy cool water of the red cooler.

Finally, the captain, in a desperate act to appear useful, suggested they troll. He fired up the engine and pushed them slowly through the water for a half-mile or more, far enough that Jim felt himself going green again. The fumes were horrible, thick with diesel stench, sticking to the layer of sunscreen lotion on his skin, filling his nostrils and eyes with the hot, sharp stink of pollution.

"Don't understand it," the captain said loudly over his shoulder. "I'm showing all kinds of activity here," he said, tapping the screen of his Doppler monitor.

"You can see fish on that thing?" Jack said, looking over the captain's shoulder.

"Well... no," Captain Ron said, giving the wheel a half-turn. For show, Jim thought. "But, here, you see that?"

The captain pointed to a gray cluster settled beneath lines and circles as it crawled slowly across the black screen.

"That's a large school of somethin' or other. Don't know what. But if this thing sees it, it's big. Like a mass of anchovies, maybe stripers..."

"So why aren't they biting?" Chris asked as he stood, walking to the wheelhouse, resting a meaty forearm against the open doorway. "You sure we're using the right bait?"

"Of course," the captain snapped, then sighed, scratching his chin. "I dunno, maybe we try different bait, maybe we try a different locale."

As the two men cornered the captain, Jim passed his eyes over the poles, hoping to see one bow, the reel to catch, the line to spring taut. He watched his dad finish his sandwich, crumple the plastic wrap in his hand, stick it into the pocket of his windbreaker. Jim smiled, feeling a rush of love for his father. He was glad they could do this together, despite it being a pretty major failure. His eyes dropped to the hold where the lone dead fish lay silent, the strange barnacles on its flesh mutating it into something bizarre, unsettling. Jim swallowed acid, swore to himself he would not partake of the meat from that one, not even if Jack gave him all the shit in the world.

Henry moved abruptly. His palms were pressed to the boat's rail, his back bent as he leaned outward, his eyes on something over the side of the boat.

Jim lurched over to his old man, put a hand on his back. "What's up, pop? See some mermaid titties?"

Henry looked at his son, smiled, and Jim smiled back, found himself wondering the last time he and his father had smiled at one another. Then Henry's smile faltered, and he pointed not to the water, but to the hull of the boat.

"You notice those before?"

Jim leaned over, put his palms down, looked to where his father pointed.

Clumped on the side of the boat, dipping in and out of the water with each slopping wave, was a wide cluster of black barnacles.

Jim bent further, looked as far over the edge as he could, and noticed a bunch of the things were stuck not only to the side of the boat but, as far as he could see through the water, down along the bottom as well.

"No..." he said, thinking back to the moment they all climbed aboard the vessel. Although, he admitted to himself, they had boarded on the other side—the starboard side, he thought—and he had been pretty out of it.

And yet...

"No," he said again, more firmly. "I didn't."

He walked, rather more steadily now, over to the other side of the boat, bent over the edge. Jack was watching him, one eyebrow arched in curiosity.

"You feeling sick, bro?"

Jim shook his head, looked over and down.

There were hundreds of them. They carpeted the side of the boat from just above the waterline and down as far as he could see. The boat being a rather sickly shade of white, it was not hard for him to gauge the coverage of the things.

"Goddamn," he said, and then Jack was at his side.

Jack bent over next to him, looked down. "Holy shit," he said, nudging his brother. "Captain needs to clean his boat, dude."

Jim shook his head, unsmiling. "No, they weren't there before. I mean, when we left."

Jack turned, sat on the edge of the boat, his bare back—he had ditched the Mello Yello shirt when the sun came out full throttle—to the water. "That's impossible, Jim. Hell, I've been looking at the walls of a jail cell for six years, but even I know those things have to stick around a while before they, you know, get shells like that. They were there, you were just too hungover to notice."

Jim saw that Jack's smile didn't make it to his brown eyes. He thought again, the memory of them boarding more clear now, defined images returning as he pulled them from the old brain rolodex, and shook his head. "No, no way." Because he did remember. The words on the side of the boat had read Not A Chance. And they'd been clean and clear as day, Jim would remember that faded shit-brown lettering the rest of his life.

And now the boat's moniker was spotted with a rash of the barnacles that had absolutely, positively, not been there that morning.

Jack stretched his arms into the air, twisted his back to let it crack, then gave Jim his most patronizing smile. "You're crazy, man. Look," he turned toward the wheelhouse, where Chris and the captain were still watching the black-and-white screen above the wheel. "Hey! Captain Ron!"

The captain turned, gave the boys an eye. "Come here and settle a bet, would you please?"

The captain killed the engine, locked the wheel. He walked over to the brothers, Chris in tow.

"If I can," he said.

Jack pointed over the side of the boat. "All that shit stuck to your fine vessel. Will you please explain to my little brother what those things are and how long they've been stuck there? He seems to think they might have just swum up like that and grabbed hold of your hull."

Jack moved aside as the captain rested his belly against the side of the boat, stared down toward the water. He was silent a moment, then another. Long enough for Jack to lose his smile.

"Sweet Jesus," he said.

And then Henry screamed.

JIM'S MOST LASTING memory of his mother as she really was—that perfect, smiling creature who was whole and happy, before they took parts of her away, before she became the pale, moaning shell she died as—was the day he and Jack had the worst fight they ever had, or, unknown to them both, ever would have.

It had been over a videogame. Jack was mercilessly destroying Jim in the newest version of Mortal Kombat, and Jim, fed up after the umpteenth defeat and sick of hearing his older brother's taunts and cackles as his fighters were disemboweled, beheaded and de-spined, stood up, his face red, and screamed, "I HATE YOU!" He followed up those eloquent words by throwing the game controller at Jack's grinning melon of a head. Mid-flight, the cable attaching the controller to the game console detached, sending its trajectory off-course, but still close enough to clip his brother right behind the ear before spinning into the basement's concrete wall, where it, rather graphically, shattered into pieces.

Jack, eyes wide in shock more than pain, put a hand to his unmarked head, then turned to see the pieces of the controller. He picked up a couple parts, looked at the broken thing, his eyes glazed. This was his controller, from his game system, which was his 16th birthday present from their parents.

"Asshole!" Jack screamed, blood rushing to his face. Jim, knowing he'd gone too far, paled, his fury washed away by switchback fear. He took a half-step toward the stairs.

"Jack," he started, but then Jack was on him. Jim screamed in pain as Jack punched him in the chest, grabbed him and pushed him hard to the thinly-carpeted floor. Jim's head bounced off the carpet that covered the concrete beneath, a white flash popping in his brain. Jim was still seeing stars as Jack pushed his face down into the coarse, mildewed carpeting.

"You dumbass! Those things are like fifty bucks!"

Jack hit him in the back of the head, spun him over and sat down hard on his sternum, knocking the wind from him while driving his knees into Jim's splayed biceps.

Jim tried to say something, to beg, to plead forgiveness, but Jack slapped him hard across the face, then thrust his palm over the top of his mouth.

As Jack pushed down, with greater and greater pressure, on Jim's lips, his fingers digging into his flushed cheeks, Jim realized, with no small amount of alarm, that Jack's hand had moved up—ever so slightly—to cover not only his mouth, but his nose as well.

Jim couldn't breathe.

Even more terrifying was the fact that Jack was not relenting, not softening his grip. No, not an inch. He wasn't yelling or cursing. Jim strained to meet his eyes with Jack's, to let him see his alarm, his terror. Because then he'll let me go, he thought. If he doesn't... if he doesn't let go...

Jack's face was bright red, his eyes bulging, his breath held, trapped deep inside. He was... moaning... and the veins in his neck stuck out as if he were the one being smothered to death, and not his smaller, weaker little brother.

Even so, it wasn't until Jim saw the silvery string of saliva slide like spider silk out of the closed corner of Jack's mouth that he felt it: terror, pure and white-hot.

He's going to kill me, he thought. He knew it was true, and he knew there wasn't a damn thing he could do about it.

Survival instincts, panic, whatever it is that makes us fight for life, kicked in with a rush. Jim bucked his hips, but Jack didn't even seem to notice. He kicked his legs, flailed his hands from the elbows down, screamed in his throat, soundlessly, using the last of his air. But nothing could break Jack from the trance. Jim tried to cry, but other than the wetness from his eyes there came only a horrible, gurgling sound from deep inside his chest.

As the tears ran and Jim stopped bucking, Jack's eyes seemed to clear, if only a little, and his mouth opened and released a PAH! sound as the breath came out.

"Jack Ransom Lowell!"

Their mother had come down the basement stairs to check on the ruckus, and now she stood, across the room from them, her hands wringing a dish towel, her face half-fury, half-fear. Her eyes, however, were blazing, and not to be denied.

Jack pulled his hand away faster than a jack-rabbit scurrying for safety, and Jim started bringing in great gulps of air, followed almost immediately by the loudest, baby-wailing sound he'd ever made, as if he were filling his lungs with air for the first time, fresh from the womb, and hating the god-awful taste of it.

"AAAAAHHHHH!" he cried, lost in the fear and the hate and the pain.

Jack leapt up, but Jim couldn't move, he was too damned spent. Exhausted from the pain of being hit, the fear of death, the fury of his own big brother... he could only lay there, crucified, wailing and screaming for his momma.

She walked over to them, stopped a foot in front of Jack, who stared at her like the most beaten dog you'd ever seen and, despite having an inch of height on her, looked every bit the caught child. Her hand whipped out and struck him across the face. The slate crack sound hovered in the air a breathless minute, then dissipated.

Their mother kneeled down, Jack a frozen statue above her, and looked at Jim. She put a hand on his hot, wet cheek.

Jim looked up at her and saw an angel. His angel. His mom. Her long blond hair fell over one side of her face, hiding a flickering brown eye. She was wearing a blue summer dress, a dark navy blue with tiny sunbursts on it. She always wore dresses, right up to the end, when they hung off of her like thin empty sacks, her frail, eaten form nothing but sharp joints, spent organs, sallow, dry hairless skin and bulbous, yellowing eyes. He pushed himself up to a sitting position, wiped his eyes and nose.

"I'm okay," he said quietly. Now that the fear had passed he felt silly for being such a baby, felt guilt at having broken the controller.

His mother nodded, stood back up, faced Jack, who hadn't moved. She gripped his chin in her hands, tilted it down to face Jim, still sitting on the floor.

"You see that?" she said, her voice sharp and irreproachable. "You see him?" Jack eyes flickered over Jim, then off again.

"Yes ma'am," he said, a hoarse whisper.

She pointed at Jim, who stood up slowly, feeling suddenly sick to his stomach. "That's all you got," she said, her voice cracking, her lip trembling. "He's all you got."

Jack's eyes widened, and he looked at her. There was fear in them. Jim looked, too, the sour lump in his stomach spreading. There were tears coming down his mother's face, and Jim couldn't understand. Not then.

"And you better protect him, Jack," she said, "because that's it. You understand? He's it."

Jack looked at his brother, questioning, fearful, his eyes wet, his hair matted with sweat.

Jim turned around and walked away slowly, wanting no more of this. He heard something and turned back, only for a moment, and saw Jack embracing his mother tightly, more tightly than he'd ever seen. He was crying into her shoulder, saying "I'm sorry, I'm sorry..." and she cried too, and stroked his head.

Jim disappeared up the stairs, but the unshakable dread went with him.


WHEN HENRY SCREAMED Jim sprang across the boat to his father, who he saw, for a split second, was bent over the side, khaki ass in the air, only the toes of his white sneakers sticking to the grimy wet floor. As he continued screaming, he flung himself backward, crashing onto his ass, his head bouncing off the edge of the red cooler.

Jim landed on his knees next to him. "Dad!"

One of Henry's hands was clutched into the opposing elbow of his windbreaker, hidden from sight. His eyes were squeezed shut, his glasses askew, his face bone pale.

"Ah... Jesus..." he stammered, eyes remaining shut tight, his mouth contorted into a grimace.

"Dad, what is it?" Jim said, gripping his father's shoulders, feeling their frailty beneath the blue jacket, almost wanting to pull them away, forget how much the old man had lost over the years.

Jack and Chris stood over Jim. The captain yelled from the wheelhouse. "What the hell happened!"

"Dad..." Jim said, and finally Henry opened his eyes. He looked up, his light blue eyes feverish, tearing with pain. He looked down at his folded arm, slowly pulled out his hand.

Stuck to the side of it, as if they'd been growing there for months, were two jet-black, acorn-sized barnacles.

"Jesus, Dad..."

Jack bent down, grabbed Henry's forearm, studied the crustaceans. "What are these things?"

Henry shook his head, then whined and shut his eyes once more. "I was reaching down, trying to grab one of them... off the boat... thought... water splashed up, a wave hit me, and there were... uh... something was in the water, like little jellyfish..." He screwed his eyes open, looked down at the crustaceans on his hand. "They're pulling my skin, Jack, they're eating my hand, I think."

"Fuck that," Jack said, looking around the boat for something, anything. A knife, a weapon.

Chris put his fingers on one of the crustaceans, tried to squeeze it. Henry screamed in pain.

"Stop!"

"Gotta pull it off, Mr. Lowell," he said, squeezing harder. "Fucking thing's like a rock."

"We need fire," Jim said. "Like a tick. We'll burn it."

"I don't think so." It was the captain, standing behind Jim now. "I have no idea how those things got on him. It's not possible, takes months for the things to secrete the shell like that. Weeks at the least..." He paused, his face a blank. He pushed the rim of his trucker cap up, scratched his forehead. "Ain't right." He looked hard at Henry, almost with suspicion, as if he were to blame for the oddity. "Ain't natural."

"How do we get them off?" Jim asked, ignoring the captain's cryptic tone.

"Well," he said, thinking, "I usually have to scrape 'em off the boat, or the pier, with a shovel. If they're on the engine, we, well, we use a jigsaw, yeah?" He positioned his hands as if he were holding a jigsaw, a similar position one might use to hold a machine gun. "But uh, here, well, that won't do."

"No," Jack said, his voice contemptuous.

"See, like I was saying earlier, they use cement, on their heads, like," the captain patted the top of his hat. "Then they secrete that shit that becomes a shell. But they don't just stick like that... takes months," he said, sounding more baffled than concerned. "If they stick to a whale, like

I said, they pull the skin up, you know, like into themselves. That way," he paused, tugged at an ear, "that way they're harder to get off."

Henry nodded. "I can feel it—oh god it hurts—I can feel them pulling my skin, they're tearing my hand up, boys! Get them off, please... Jack, get them off me."

Jack nodded, turned to Chris. "Pull it."

Jim felt the pinging bells of alarm in his head, but he said nothing. He watched his father's eyes go wide with terror.

Chris pinched two strong fingers onto one of the barnacles. Henry's face flushed. "Wait..." he said.

Chris pulled. Like one might pull a Band-Aid that had been superglued to your skin.

The thing came off with a puckering squelch, and Henry threw his head back and screamed.

Chris held the thing up, showing them. There were thin strips of flesh hanging from the base of it. From the crown, where it opened slightly, fiber-thin tentacles were wriggling, reaching. Just like the sea bass, Jim thought.

"Get rid of it," Jack said, his voice steady.

Chris tossed the thing over the side into the water.

Henry, still screaming, kicking his feet, his body lying in a half-inch of dirty sea water, held his hand high into the air. They could all see the blood trickling down his arm, the quarter-sized hole left by the thing's removal—a wet, bright red fleshy wound that emptied blood down his arm and to the deck of the boat in trickling spurts.

"Jesus..." the captain said, a hand over his mouth. "I'll get the first aid kit."

Jim sat down, put his arm around his father. Henry collapsed into him, rested his head on Jim's thighs, all but weeping openly, his hand a bloody mess.

Jack looked fixedly at his father, his face emotionless, his eyes cold. Jim tried to meet his eye, to beg him to hold off, to give it a second, but Jack's eyes were hard and clear as they studied Henry's wounded hand, his thin, crying frame.

Jim didn't feel like he knew this man. This version of Jack. This was a brother he'd never met, the one who'd done all that time in Lancaster, the one who made it through, who survived whatever heartbreaking atrocities he'd been subjected to over the six years in state prison. Jim was afraid, but also comforted. This version of Jack could make decisions Jim had no interest in making.

Jim rested his palms on his father's head, felt a swelling bump on the back where he must have cracked it into the metal cooler. What a mess, he thought.

Jack looked at Henry's face another moment, then his eyes dropped to the other barnacle stuck to the bleeding hand, an inch away from the last, harbored like a black lump on the webbing between the thumb and forefinger. He looked at Chris, who was already reaching.

"Now the other one."

HENRY GROANED AS the captain slathered his hand in ointment, then wrapped it tightly in gauze. The cuff of his windbreaker was stiff with dried blood, his face deathly white, the sagging mouth twitching and grimacing with the pain.

The three younger men stood by stupidly, watching. Jim finally sat down, looked out at the water. The sun hovered past its zenith, heading away from them now, toward the edge of the horizon, the crest of the waves streaked with shimmering gold.

As his father moaned and the captain talked about getting the boat in as quickly as possible, Jim thought to look over the side once more, curious as to how the passive crustaceans could have so quickly mounted themselves to his father's hand. A freak thing, he thought.

He was careful to keep his hands up on the side rail, his fingers resting on the all but worn-through strips of coarse adhesive made to give one tread while walking along the outside of the boat. He leaned over... then jerked away, almost stumbling backward. He spun around, looked at the men, his eyes darting between them.

"Jack," he said, his voice high-pitched and panicked.

Jack studied Jim's gawping face, then walked over, stood close. "What is it Jimmy?"

Jim nodded toward the side of the boat. "Take a look, man. I think something's wrong."

Jack's brows arched in on each other, and he stepped past Jim and looked. After a moment, having overheard them, Chris joined Jack at the side of the boat. Jim waited, hoping against hope they would not see what he'd seen, that he'd somehow got it wrong, misread things.

"What the hell?" Chris said, and Jim knew he wasn't wrong. That they were in trouble. He joined them, looked again, and swallowed a scream.

The boat was alive.

Blue, black and white hard-shelled barnacles now covered the boat right up to the bulwark, mere inches from where their hands rested. The sides and front were heavy with dense layers of the crustaceans. The black acorn-shaped ones, but more than that. There were wriggling, pulsing starfish-shaped, semi-translucent creatures settled among them, as if fighting for space. Jim noticed, in some spots, there were slick-brown tubes probing, seeking someplace to settle themselves into the thickening carpet of organisms.

Jim bent over further, could see that the spread of sea creatures continued to mass even more so below sea level. He imagined that from below the boat must look like a heavy black beard, growing longer by the second, a living coral-rock floating along the surface of the vast ocean, getting heavier by the minute.

But it's been barely an hour, he thought, thinking of when he last looked over the boat. Hasn't it? It's not possible. It's just not... His mind raced, desperate for answers that made sense, that would bring logic back to the equation, that would help him find some small piece of sanity to build upon, to steady his mind and allow for rational thought.

None of them spoke for a moment, all of them seeking that equilibrium, that rationale. As if struck with a new fear, Jack groaned and moved quickly to the back of the boat, toward the engine. Chris, having the same thought, joined him.

Jim could only stand and stare at the wet boards of the deck, wondering how all of this had gone so terribly, terribly wrong.

"Oh no," Chris said under his breath.

Jim, needing to know the worst now, went over, looked down at the giant rudder resting just below the surface.

The rudder was gone, covered in a white organic mass of barnacles and rope-thick tentacles, a balled-up writhing sphere of featureless crustaceans.

Stepping back, Jim saw, with a sharp pang of terror, that a few of the creatures had settled among the metal pole rods and were now staggered along the handrail.

My God, Jim thought, they're on the boat.

"What's wrong with you boys?" the captain said, stomping past Jim and shouldering Chris aside. Jack and Chris stepped back, not wanting to see anymore. They watched the captain as he looked over the edge, saying nothing.

Abruptly, he cursed and turned, his face crimson, his mouth fixed in a hard line. He pushed past them, stomping back toward the wheelhouse.

"Damn damn DAMN!" he yelled, then, with more dexterity than Jim would have thought him able, he hoisted himself up onto the coaming of the boat's side, grabbed the rail that ran the top-length of the wheelhouse, and skirted the outside of the boat toward the bow, where Jim had seen a small seating deck for two or three that none of them had bothered to yet occupy.

A few moments later he came sliding back toward them, along the other side, casting glances downward as he smothered his belly against the standing shelter of the wheelhouse, shuffling along and huffing with exertion. He stepped down and bent over, panting. When he looked up at them, Jim thought he saw tears in his eyes.

"They've covered my whole boat," he said, shaken. "Past the spray rail, right up to the goddamn sheerline. I don't know..."

He removed his hat, his matted hair stringy and dirty beneath like white seaweed, spotted patches of his broad pate shining through the tangles. "I just don't fucking know..." he said miserably.

Jim wondered if the old salty captain was gonna have himself a little breakdown right there and then. Have a good long cry and hug himself, think about all the whores he'd never lay, all the tobacco he'd never smoke, all the whiskey he'd never drink, while his mind snapped like dry kindling in a fire and he rocked and drooled while the rest of them were left to deal with the boat, his injured father and the sea monstrosities that were surrounding them in greater and greater numbers by the second.

"Captain Ron," Jim started. "We need to do some..."

The captain snapped his head up, his magnified eyes blazing and sharp. His hands were clenched into fists. "Shut up, boy! Just shut the fuck up!" he yelled, spittle flying from his mouth. "You want to know what's going on, well guess what, school-boy? I have no fucking clue what's going on!" He smashed one giant paw into the side of the boat.

They all stood, silent, waiting. Wondering if this is where someone else would have to take control. Mutiny, Jim thought wildly, and had to suppress the image of pulling a sword from a rusted scabbard and holding it to the captain's throat.

The captain turned back on them before he could continue the fantasy. His face calm once more, his voice now suddenly steady, suddenly firm. "Look boys, your daddy, well, yeah, he's injured, and my boat, as you can see, is taking on a lot of organic weight."

He looked to the sky, the sun halfway home, the day still hot, the brightness more honey than sunflower now, aging toward death as they rocked on the waves.

"It's time to get you boys home," he said, and no one argued.

Committed now, he moved quickly, quietly. Went from rod to rod, pulling them down, stowing them sloppily along the deck. He secured them with two bungee cords, then went back to the controls, started the engine. His head cocked up to the Doppler screen. He shook his head, flipped a switch and turned the key.

The engine roared. The underwater rumbling of the propeller starting up vibrated the deck beneath their feet. Jim sat down, palms flat on the worn canvas of the bench, careful to keep his back from touching the rail. Jack put his t-shirt back on, and Chris—quite gently, Jim thought— helped Henry off the floor and onto the padded bench lining the opposite side of the deck.

Jim could hear Henry's moans as the boat's engine screamed like an animal, the exhaust washing over them like a cancerous dragon's dying breath. Jim was able to make out the captain saying, "Come on, come on..."

There was a choking eruption from beneath the boat. Jim was sure the hull was being torn to pieces. The propeller cracked so loudly Henry covered his ears, wincing at the pain in his bandaged hand. It sounded caught, and as the rotor tried desperately to muscle the propeller to action there was a whining so shrill it filled the air like locust wings, so loud now that they were all covering their ears.

"Come ON!" the captain roared.

There came a sharp pop, a loud belching sound from beneath the deck, and the boat shook as if slapped by the tail of a great whale. The sounds of the engine hummed more quietly, then sputtered, then died.

With an almost eerie calm, Jim watched smoke pour up from all sides of the boat. A wet smoke, thick and black and carrying upwards, past them, toward the clouds. For a moment—a brief moment—he couldn't see the ocean, and was almost grateful. His eyes stung with the sooty dying breath of the vessel and he looked upward. He saw that the sun, lightly-veiled by the cloudy gray wall, was turning a deep shade of crimson, growing darker with every passing second.

The captain slammed a hand against the controls, tried vainly to start the engine once more.

There was only silence. The captain spun, his calm eyes gone now, his hard-set mouth open and wet, his cheeks bright red. He pointed a finger at the Doppler screen.

"The water's filled with 'em!" he yelled, decorum gone, leadership driven out by a fear approaching madness. "They're everywhere!"

Jack stood up and eyeballed the monitor. Jim could see from where he sat that the little screen was filled with a massive white blob, extending from one edge to the other.

"What does this mean?" Jack said, running his fingertip from one end of the digitized white mass to the other. "I... how much does this cover? Can we row out of it? Get to better water?"

The captain looked at Jack like he was the Mad Hatter himself, sprung from the storybook to chase the captain's sanity far away.

"Captain Ron!" Jack snapped, his voice a whip. "Can we row out of this?"

The captain seemed to steady, to calm himself. He put his hat back on, took off his glasses and wiped at his eyes roughly. He took a deep, shuddering breath.

"Okay," he said, and stepped onto the deck. The black smoke of the blown engine wispy now, the ocean visible once more, waiting patiently from all around them for their next ridiculous maneuver. "Okay," he repeated, more loudly this time. He addressed Jack, but spoke loudly enough for them all to hear.

"Imagine a dining room table, right? A nice white tablecloth on it, it's Thanksgiving, whatever..."

Jim and Jack shared a quick what the hell? glance as only two brothers can do, but didn't interrupt.

"Okay, so there's a bunch of you eating, yeah? Nice big table. Now, imagine you put an almond in the middle of that table. Nothin' else, it's all white and clean. But there's that almond, and you're all sitting around looking at the stupid little brown nut. You got me?"

Jack said nothing. They were all staring at the captain now, waiting for some guidance, some sense to come from all of this strangeness.

"That table?" he said, meeting each of their faces. "That's the amount of ocean you see on that little screen there. Right? Okay, now that almond?" He looked at Jim, then Henry. "That's us.

"We ain't paddlin' out of this, fellas. We ain't no way getting away from whatever the hell this is. It's like the ocean farted something wicked, and we're sitting right on her asshole."

Chris snorted at this, and, incredibly, even Henry smiled. Jack paced from one side of the boat to the other, mind racing for solutions.

"Ain't this pretty as a peach..." the captain mumbled, lost in his own mind.

Jim stared out at the water. Saw the flashes of sunlight in the crevices of each wave, the incredible breadth of its body. He strained his eyes, stared closely at the calmer patches of the surface. Did he see the cloudy dust of shapes filling each wave, or was he imagining it? Imagining what his brain was afraid to see but, in a twisted way, wanted to see? To see that the water was filled with billions of micro-sized creatures, gelatinous but alive, swimming, floating, waiting for something to latch onto, somewhere to live, somewhere to feed.

He looked away, sickened, felt himself shaking. He put his head in his hands, willed the images to stop. If imagination was truly an invisible organ given to humans by God, like he'd once read, so that they might better understand Him, then Jim would have liked to have ripped the fucking thing out and thrown it into the sea right there and then.

Because we fear the incomprehensible, we fear other life, he thought reflectively, recalling a lesson on evolution from high school. It's defensive... the alpha species always looking over their shoulder, always afraid of what might come next in the chain...

"What about radio?" Jack said abruptly, breaking Jim's thoughts. "A beacon? Whatever. Can we get help to come to us?"

The captain nodded. "Yeah, sure," he said, sighing heavily. "I... I wasn't expecting... but this is bad, yeah. I'll get on the radio, start putting through an S.O.S. I'll hit my emergency beacon. Coast Guard should be here within an hour, I'd imagine. Assuming..."

The captain turned and went into the wheelhouse. He flipped open a small plastic cover, pushed a fat red button. Then he grabbed a mic from an overhead radio, flipped it on, and began relaying coordinates into it, steady and calm as you pleased.

Jim grabbed Jack's arm lightly. "Assuming what?"

Jack frowned, but met his brother's eyes. "Assuming we're the only ones in trouble."

As the captain radioed for help, the visible part of the emergency beacon strobed in a steady rhythm, bright-white flickers of light from the top of the wheelhouse settled below a massive, swaying antenna that flexed upward, silently beckoning for rescue.

Jim went to his father, pulled at his arm, studied the gauzed hand. "You holding up, pop?"

Henry nodded and Jim slumped down next to him. He fought the overwhelming urge to rest his head on his dad's shoulder, so his father could do what he had done when Jim was just a kid with a scraped knee, a bee sting or had been abruptly woken from a nightmare, put an arm around him and tell him things would be okay, that he was safe.

"This isn't the trip we planned, I guess." Henry said lightly, a faint, sickly smile on his face.

Jim shook his head. "No, but at least we're together again. And that's something."

"Ayuh," Henry said, nodding. "It's been real good to see you and your brother together. Last night," he coughed, his voice disturbingly weak, so quiet Jim could barely hear it above the stubborn waves and the captain's steady calls of Mayday. "Last night," he continued, "I was watching you guys. You know, during the game. Yeah, I was in and out a bit, but who could sleep through all that noise?"

Jim smiled, nodded. "Just like old times."

"Yeah," his father said, wistfully. "You know, your mother and I..." He stopped, as if gathering himself, sifting through the memories, categorizing away the landmines a road of memories lay down, each wrong step triggering the emotional damage all over again. "We would sit upstairs, at the dinner table, drinking coffee... or Bailey's, or both!" he said, with a laugh. "We'd listen to you guys in the basement, yelling and screaming at the television, demanding the Kings win one... we'd just... sit there. We wouldn't talk at all. Every... well, every now and then we'd look at each other and sorta smile, just enjoying all the life coming from down those stairs, all that nervous energy, the joy... the joy when the guys scored one. The exuberance."

Jim didn't know what to say. His mother was not a topic they spoke of, rarely if not never, and his stomach soured at the confessional nature of his father's words.

Henry gripped Jim's hand in his own good one, pulled

him closer to him. Jim lowered his head on his dad's bony shoulder, looked over and saw Jack staring at them both from across the deck, his face a blank.

"The hardest part of losing someone..." Henry said in a whisper, then sighed, a deep-down pain in his voice. "Please understand, what I did after... the way I was. The way I am. It's not the losing that hurt me the most, son..." He paused, patted the top of Jim's head, gave a weary sigh. "It was the damned going on."

Henry let go of Jim's arm, and Jim sat up, head bowed as Henry continued. "That's what eats you up from the inside. A little bit every day," he said. "Just like it did your mother."

Jim said nothing a moment, then put an arm around his father's thin shoulders, gave him a gentle squeeze. "I know, pop. It's okay."

As he embraced him, Jim's eyes wandered past his father, toward the rear of the boat.

A broken line of dark barnacles had now taken root along the bow's washboard. He frowned, then twisted to look behind them, down toward the water, and could swear the rail of the boat sat closer to the surface of the ocean than it had only minutes ago.

At least a couple feet closer, he thought numbly. And there's no way in seven hells that's a good thing.

"I'm not feeling well, son," Henry said, rather too loudly, as if pained. "I think I better lie down."

Jim stood, gave his father the bench. Henry lifted his legs and let himself lay down like a toddler taking an afternoon nap.

"Are you warm? Do you want to take off your jacket?" Jim said, eyeing the blood-stained cuffs.

"No, actually, I'm a little chilly. Wind must be picking up. Probably just a bit seasick." Henry closed his eyes.

Jim didn't feel any wind. Felt only a light warm breeze with the faintest threat of a chill wisping through it.

Jack and Chris were digging through the cooler. Jack pulled out two cans of beer, handed one to Chris. They cracked them, tapped cans, and drank heavily.

"Any more?" Jim asked, not really wanting it but wanting something.

"Last two, buckaroo," Chris said, then held his out. "Happy to share."

Jim shook his head, looked at the water, the sky, his jailbird brother drinking beer with his best friend, Henry already breathing steady, the captain in his shelter whispering sweet need into the radio mic. Best settle in, he reasoned.

There was a loud CRACK from beneath the boat, like a tree-branch splitting from the trunk. The boat tremored and the captain came running from the wheelhouse.

"The hell was that?" he said, looking at the others like they were to blame.

Jack squatted on the deck, placed the palm of a hand on the flat ruddy wood. "I think..."

There was a loud belch, and all eyes went to Chris.

"I think your boat is breaking, Captain," Chris said, and chugged the last of the last beer.

A HALF-HOUR WENT by, and no Coast Guard. Jim, needing space, hopped up alongside the wheelhouse, dared to walk along the outside of the boat. He shuffled along the three-inch coaming while gripping the railing that ran atop the wheelhouse before dropping down in the stern. It was nicer up here. Tight, but dry and clean. He settled onto one of the cushions, tried to ignore the memory of what was growing all around them, under them, layers upon layers of something from the deep ocean, something sinister, something parasitic.

He twisted his body. It was colder now and he'd already put his black hoodie on. He stared at the setting sun and listened to the steady breathing of the countless waves. The sunset looked massive, a large, bulbous ball of gas set to explode like a red bomb, break apart all over the world, erase them all with fire.

He laid down, closed his eyes. After a few moments, exhaustion took him, and he fell asleep.

HIS MOTHER WAITED for him in a dream. She was not young, not healthy, not beautiful. She had death inside her.

She lay in her hospital bed, tubes running in and out of her so many places he couldn't count. She'd been subjected to a third operation, a third mad attempt for—if not salvation—an elongation of her life... a third try.

A third failure.

He stood next to her bed. They were alone. Her hair was gone, her eyes deep black sockets, her cheekbones sharp and protruding beneath her yellowed plastic-wrap skin.

"Jimmy?" she said. So faint, so weak.

He went to her. Held her frail hand that felt like sticks wrapped in tissue paper. "Yeah," he said, trying to smile.

She wasn't looking at him. She was looking at the tubes in her arms. "What are they putting into me, Jimmy? What is all this?"

He looked at the tubes, filling her with fluids, painkillers, medicine, whatever-the-fuck they gave to dying mothers.

"You need it," he said, trying for a tone of confidence. "It's for the pain, mainly."

She shook her head, lifted it from the pillow. He could see the stain on the case where she had sweat poison. "No..." she said, lifting her hands high into the air and the tubes extending with them. She looked like a featherless bird inspecting its broken wings. "No," she repeated. "They're putting something inside me, Jimmy. I don't want it. It's filling me up, I can... I can feel it." She twitched her face toward him and stared at him with those dead black eyes. "I can feel it in my stomach," she moaned.

They'd removed so much of his mother's intestines he was frankly surprised the stomach was still fillable with anything. She certainly wasn't eating solid food anymore, had no appetite for it. She couldn't keep it down anyway. Besides, her teeth had fallen out, her lips were black and hard, crusted with dry flakes.

When had that happened? he thought.

She pushed his hand away, reached for the thin hospital sheet with the baby-blue teardrop pattern, pushed it aside, revealed her skinny body draped within a stained gown the color of dead skin. Jim noticed a large wet patch by her crotch.

"Mom," he said, feeling sick, "let me get someone."

"No!" she yelled, with more force and will than he would have thought remained in her. "Noooo," she wailed, "look at these goddamn tubes, Jimmy! What are they doing to me?"

He eyed the cluster of tubes, followed them from her body to the IV bags hanging by her bed. He took half-a-step toward the rack that held three, four of the bags, hanging there like rotting fruit from a tree. He narrowed his eyes at one of the bags feeding into his mother's right arm.

The liquid inside was clear, but... there was something. He looked closer, his nose almost touching the sterile plastic of the bag's exterior. Something, thousands of somethings, were floating inside the bag. Like dust motes caught in sunshine.

"Well that doesn't seem right," he mumbled, resting a hand gently on the bag.

The dust motes floated gracefully toward his touch. He watched, fascinated, as they migrated—as one— toward the palm of his hand on the other side of the plastic. He watched as they clumped, could almost feel the weight of them, pushing against the bag, reaching for his skin.

He pulled his hand away, frightened and sick. He watched, repulsed, as the clumps separated, spread themselves out evenly once more. He saw them drift down the IV tube, diving with each drip into his mother's veins.

"Jimmy," she cried suddenly, snapping his attention back to her. "Something's wrong!" He started to reach for her hand, but she was sitting up now, clawing at the exposed flesh of arms, her knees, her thighs.

"Mom."

She grabbed the hem of her gown, pulled it up over her crotch, exposing herself. Jim gasped, horrified and unsure how to stop her from whatever she was doing.

Unable to stop himself, he stared down at her, at her bone-thin thighs, the skin blotchy and flabby where it fell away from the thick meat of muscle that was now gone forever. Her crotch was hairless below a distended belly that had swollen to the size of a soccer ball. How had he not noticed that? And where the fuck were the nurses in this hospital?

He grabbed a call button tethered to the side of the bed rail, began pressing it frantically.

"Hello!" he yelled, his own voice dying in the small, air-tight room.

She clawed at her belly, rubbed at it frantically, her hands folded over, the flesh seared into hard fins. She was trying to push the thing out.

"Jimmy, help me!" she screamed, her voice raspy and breathless. "Get it out!"

Jim ran to the door, tried to open it. It wouldn't budge. He kicked it, looked at the window leading to the hallway but saw nothing but inky black, as if they were miles underneath the surface of the darkest ocean.

"Jimmy?" she said, and he turned.

Her eyes were solid coals, her skin mottled with open, oozing pores and blackened patches of dead flesh. She opened her mouth, pushed a white crab-like creature out instead of a tongue, gummed it. She pushed down on her swollen belly and it caved inward. He heard a gushing sound. Dirty seawater flowed over the edge of the bed. Heavier things floating within it slapped as they hit the floor.

He stepped away from the rush of water, could see the gelatinous shapes swimming in the liquid, splashing across the floor. He looked up at her once more, saw her eyes were crusted over, heavy, blinded.

She reached clawed hands, like those of a sickly, fleshy crab, toward him.

"Mom?" he said, felt a chill racing up his back.

"HELP ME!" she screamed, and reached one deformed hand to her tongue, ripped the thing out, dropped it, looked at him with a mouthful of blood and sea.

The windows exploded inward. The ocean rushed in, filled the room. He had a moment to gasp in a last breath as his feet lifted from the floor. The room filled to the ceiling and he dared not breathe. The water was cluttered with debris but clear and deep blue.

His mother's body rose from the bed and floated upward, pale and white like a broken angel, her gown flowing around her like a ray's cape. With a thrusting jerk of her bony legs, she surged toward him, her black acorn eyes never leaving his own.

The cold slick flesh of her mutated hands went around his head and she pushed her mouth onto his and he gagged and choked and convulsed as his lungs flooded. Her icy blood-blackened fluid flowed down his throat and filled him.

JIM JERKED AWAKE, the nightmare evaporating, his skin crawling with damp chill. He shivered, wrapped his hoodie closer around him, his head heavy, his eyes pressed inward by invisible pressures. His mouth was pasty and dry and his stomach felt twisted and tight, his guts sour. No more puking, he ordered himself.

He pushed himself up off the sodden cushion of the small bench, felt his back twinge from having lain at the odd angle... how long? He worked his jaw, rubbed at one eye that had been pressed into the thin coarse fabric.

It was dark. Well, darker. He turned his head, grimaced at the crick in his neck, saw the sun dipped low in the bloody water, its innards spilling out onto the surface of the ocean, sliced open cleanly by the horizon. The waves lapped at the side of the boat, slapping carelessly against the hull as the boat rose and dipped, creaky as an old ghost pushing a rocker.

He stopped to listen. There was something else. Grunting. Exertions. He heard Jack curse softly, carried away by the wind before he could hear the words that followed.

Jim gathered his wits, halting, resentfully remembering their situation. He tried to will it away into a bad dream, but reality washed over him despite his efforts.

He looked over the front edge of the boat, not sure what to expect... but there was no more boat. Not anymore.

The entire shell of the vessel was covered ass-to-lips in... what? Barnacles? Crabs? What was it? Too dark to see clearly now, but there was a lot of movement among the rocky black crust that had thickened along the side of the small vessel. Shuddering violently from the cold, from disgust, from fear, he carefully shuffled to the front of the standing shelter that divided the boat. He looked through the grimy windows. The wheelhouse was empty.

He could see shapes, however, toward the bow. Bodies standing, struggling. He pulled himself up, gripped the cold handrail that ran along the top of the shelter, began the shuffle-step back along the side of the boat toward the rear deck. The wind whipped up in a sudden frenzy, blew his hood off his head and his foot slipped. There was a crunch as his heel dug into the black crustaceans that covered the surface of the boat. He pulled it up quickly, shook it to be sure nothing had stuck, then continued quickly toward the bow.

Climbing down onto the deck, the first thing he saw was his father's frail form, lying where he'd left him, on the bench along the starboard side of the deck. His eyes were open and his head lifted. He was reaching with one hand...

The soles of Jim's shoes smacked the wet deck. He looked from his father to Jack and Chris, who were at the other side of the boat, their backs to him. They had been moving, struggling. Now they froze.

Jack turned, his eyes wide and stark in the gloaming light. He looked at Jim for a blank moment, said nothing, then turned back.

Jim looked into the wheelhouse, then to his father, then back to Jack and Chris. Something was off. His sleep-addled brain wasn't making all the connections, he was still fuzzy, thirsty, so thirsty. He thought of grabbing an ice cube from the cooler, sucking on it.

The captain. Where was Captain Ron? The thought

struck him like a bolt of energy, snapping his mind to attention. He took a couple steps toward Jack and Chris.

"Boys, please..." he heard his father say weakly, insignificantly.

Jim reached his brother's side. He and Chris were holding a thick rope. They both wore gloves, rubber gloves that Jim knew they didn't bring with them. He looked down, toward the thing they were... lifting? dropping?

Captain Ron.

The lower half of the captain's body was submerged in the icy sea. The upper part was dry, and unconscious. They had strapped a life vest to him, pulled the rope through behind the shoulders, and were now lowering him into the water. His trucker hat was nowhere in sight.

"Jack?"

"Not now, Jimmy," his brother said, snarling under the strain of his effort.

Jim looked at their stressed, serious faces, then down at the captain. He could think of nothing that would help this make sense. Nothing that, as far as he could figure, would help him better understand the situation. He crossed his arms, tried to warm himself.

"What's wrong with him?" was what he ended up with, hoping the answer would clarify things, shed some light on the strange scene he'd stepped into.

"He's dead, Jimmy," Jack said, and the captain lowered a few inches more, so that now only his shoulders and head were above the water, buoyed somewhat by the life vest.

"I don't..."

"Jim," his father said.

Jim turned, and his father beckoned him with his good hand. Jim went to him, sat down, feeling more assured about things when his father sat up as well, leaned against him lightly.

"Captain Ron had a, well... a stroke? A heart attack? Something. He just kind of yelled out, then collapsed, right here in front of us. He was pacing, angry. Angry that..." Henry licked his lips, gathered his strength, then continued. "Angry that no one had come, see?"

His father looked into his eyes. Jim noticed they looked a bit wild, a bit haggard. *Mad*, a voice screamed inside his head. *He looks fucking bat-shit insane, Jimmy!* Jim shook his head, cleared the voice, looked down at the deck.

"Stroke?" he said.

Henry nodded, his tongue rolling along his lips. "Yeah, that's right. A stroke. And he was dead, son. Dead as anything. No pulse, nothing. Chris, see, Chris, he tried, tried to, uh, revive him. But nothing would bring him back, you could see it. You could see he was dead. You were asleep, you were upfront, asleep."

Jim thought a moment, trying to gather himself, gather the facts. It was all so surreal, it almost made sense.

"So why are they putting him in the water?" he asked quietly. "Are they burying him at sea or something?"

His father nodded, looked at the two other men, his thin hair falling across his forehead into rapidly blinking eyes.

"No help is coming," Henry said, "And... and he got really angry about it. Real upset. No help, no Coast Guard, no response on the radio, and then..."

His father looked away, as if ashamed. Jim stared at him. "Then what?"

Henry twisted around, stared ice blue insanity into his son's eyes. Jim hardly recognized him, this thin, old, crazy man sitting next to him on a broken boat in the deep reaches of the ocean. "Something went wrong with the radio, Jimmy. See, the bottom of the boat is flooding, we think. Slowly, the, uh, the hull is cracked, or something. The weight is too much." He grabbed Jim's forearm with his good hand, the strength of his grip frightening. Jim fought every repulsive instinct to pull away from that touch. "We're sinking, son."

Jim stood, took his arm from his father's cold, hard fingers. He paced, the adrenaline of fear slamming through his veins. "No, no way. Sinking?"

Henry nodded, the tiredness seeping back into his face. Jim waited for him to lie down again.

"So what the hell are they doing with Captain Ron? Losing weight? It can't make that much of a difference!"

"We ain't losing weight," he heard Jack say in response. Jim turned, could see the men were now bent over, straining even harder. My God, he thought, they're bringing him back up!

And they were.

After a few minutes of huffing and the sick sounds of flesh scraping roughly against the layer of crustaceans that covered the shell of the boat, the two men had the captain's body nearly raised. Jim stood for a better view, could see his giant lolling head looking blindly up at the stars.

"Damn it!" Chris yelled, and the rope whistled and

the captain vanished. There was a loud splash, and another sharp wave of nausea stabbed Jim in the guts.

"I've got him!" Jack said through clenched teeth, the ropey muscles in his neck straining with effort.

Chris quickly pulled his end tight again, and after a few more minutes of cussing and grunting the men pulled the captain's obese body back onto the ship. With a last heave, they dragged him over the edge and dropped him. His seawater-soaked body flopped onto the deck with a loud smack, and laid still. Water oozed out from under him, as if he were made of ocean and it was leaking from holes in his skin.

Jack and Chris, still wearing the strange gloves, pushed the body as far into a corner as they could, keeping him clear of the main floor of the deck.

Jack took off the gloves, and Chris followed suit. They dropped them onto a bench. Chris sat heavily on the cooler. Jack walked over to Jim, his eyes as sane as a priest's.

"Jim," he said, smoothly and calmly. "Like Dad said, this boat is sinking. It's breaking apart, been getting lower and lower in the water for the last couple hours while you've been shut-eye. No one's come. No one's reached out on the radio. The captain, like Dad told ya, he just..." Jack shrugged, shook his head. "He just fucking dropped dead." He paused, let out a breath, lifted his arms to his sides helplessly, let them fall to his hips. "And so here we are. No radio, no help, boat's sinking. What's left?"

Jack studied the horizon, not knowing what to say, what to do. This was all beyond him now.

"The water, brother," Jack said. "If no help comes soon, we're gonna have to swim."

Jim thought about this, impressed with how calm he felt, how at least now they had a plan. And really, how far out from shore could they be? A few miles? Hell, they could all get life vests and float if they got tired. Yeah, sure, they could definitely swim. They would make it. Of course they would.

"One problem," Jack said, wriggling his fingers in the air. "The fishies."

Jack's calm began to fissure. "Fishies?"

"The shit, man," Jack said. "The barnacles, whatever the fuck is all over this boat. It's in the water, too. You've seen it, I know you have. So have we. The water's filled with the little fuckers. All around, all beneath us." He paused, rubbed at his face. "We'd have to swim right through it."

Jim nodded, still feeling that calm, but it was laced now. Laced with a deep, rising fear. Was it panic? Perhaps, perhaps... it was possible that somewhere, down in his subconscious, he knew they were all going to die.

Yes, perhaps, perhaps his mind was somehow... shielding him from this knowledge. Keeping it at bay for the moment. Protecting his sanity. A survival instinct. Of course we'll live, Jim thought. Because shit like this? Shit like this doesn't happen. Not really. Not to normal folks like us. It just doesn't happen.

"So," Jim said, his throat dry and suddenly sore, "the captain? You're... what?"

"Testing," Jack said. "Wanna see what these things will do to flesh. We've seen how they gripped onto Dad, but maybe, the ones in the water, maybe... I don't know, maybe they won't have a taste for us."

Silently, without Jim noticing, Chris had stood and

moved a few feet from them. He was watching them. Jim thought, just maybe, that Chris was watching him. Seeing how he'd react. Making sure he didn't freak out, go nuts. Because then you'd feel a pain in the back of your head, Jim. A hard pain and the lights would go out. Then it'd be you next. Dipping time for Jimmy, into the cold sea, into the mass of the jelly fishies. You'd be the feast, then, Jimmy.

He took a half-step back, toward his father, away from Jack and Chris. "Okay," he said. "We'll wait then?"

Jack nodded, and Chris sat his massive bulk down onto the cooler once more. He was a broad, dark shadow, his back leaned against the wheelhouse, his head tilted back... but the whites of his eyes were lowered, watching.

"That's right, little brother, we wait." Jack said, reaching out and squeezing Jim's shoulder. "Don't worry," he said, "I'll get you home safe." He smiled and the whites of his teeth were phosphorescent against the dying sky. "I promise."

CHRIS WAS THE one who found the hatch that led to a small, waist-high cabin below the wheelhouse.

"It's where we found the gloves," he explained when he pulled it open, revealing the black maw beneath. "It's beginning to get wet down there, so I'm gonna bring everything we can use up here." Jim stood by while Chris shone the dingy-brown beam of a found waterproof flashlight into the hold.

Jim looked down, followed the trace of the beam. He saw some boxes, the bottoms now dark with moisture.

There was a mass of blankets on a narrow army mattress, likely where the captain slept it off when he stayed out overnight.

"There's more than these gloves," Chris said, almost excited with the thrill of digging through someone else's life, of trespassing. "There's suits. You know, rubbers."

"Rubbers?" Jim said, eyeing the filthy cot.

"Suits, man," Chris said. "Like, whatever, rain gear. Hold on."

Chris dropped below. Jim could only see the flashlight beam and the dark curve of Chris's hunched back as he dug through the debris of the captain's former life.

"Jesus, do you need that many porn mags?" Chris said, his voice dull and deep within the hold. "Here!"

Jim started as a yellow rubber suit was thrust up at him.

"Take it," Chris said, already pushing the beam at other parts of the cabin. "Put it to the side. I'm gonna hand you more stuff."

Following directly behind was a second rubber suit— including a wide-brimmed hat, jacket, pants and boots. Next came a couple single-serving boxes of cereal, an open box of granola bars, and a plastic jug of water, the sight of which made Jim's parched mouth salivate.

"Oh yeah," Chris said, his breath coming harsh and fast. "Shit man, the water's really coming in. Take this, I'm coming up."

A large, rusted metal can came up from below. The base was rounded and it had a spout and a rough handle. Jim grappled with it, the heavy fluid sloshing around inside causing him to nearly lose his balance before he lifted it over the lip of the hatch and slid the thing onto the deck.

It reeked of gas.

Chris climbed up, lifted the large hatch shut and let it slam down. "Gasoline?" Jim said.

Jack came over from across the deck, where he had been talking quietly with their father.

"Great," Jack said. "Extra fuel for a broken engine."

Chris dusted himself off, looking closely at his legs with the flashlight, inspecting them. Looking for fishies, the voice in Jim's head thought with a chuckle.

"You all right?" Jack asked Chris, the slightest tinge of concern in his voice.

"Yeah man, I'm fine!" Chris snapped. "Just don't want those things on me."

"No..." Jack said, pausing a moment for emphasis until they were both looking at him. "You don't."

Jack took the light from Chris's hand, turned and walked to the other side of the deck where the dead captain lay.

He shone the light at the body.

Jim, ironically remembering the captain's very instructions, ran immediately for the side of the boat and puked up whatever remained of his semi-digested sandwich and beer.

"Don't get too close to that edge," Jack said loudly, and Jim pulled himself up, removed his hands from the rail. He noticed barnacles had crept up and lined the length of the bulwark, dotting the rim of the boat's edge.

"Shit," Jim said, spitting. He turned back, saw Chris kneeling, Jack holding the light.

The captain was covered in them. Head-to-toe.

Some white hair was visible, sticking out between two

hardened black shells where his head should be. Something tube-like wiggled near his belly, seeking purchase.

Jack moved the light from one end of the captain to the other, the glistening wet ebony of the crustaceans reflecting back at him like hateful eyes. Tentacles moved in and out of the shells all along the corpse, and the great belly appeared to be swelling and sinking, as if the old man were still breathing under there.

Jim held the thought a moment, tried to let it go, couldn't. "Jack..." he said, quietly, fearfully.

"I know, man," he said. "It's gross."

"Jack," Jim repeated, taking a step back toward his brother and Chris, the lifelong bodyguard. "Jack, you guys... I mean, the captain..."

Jack turned the beam of the light, shone it into Jim's face, blinding him.

"What about him?" Jack's voice came cool and steady from the dark beyond the beam.

"Jack, please tell me... he was dead, right?"

Jack lowered the beam, stared at Jim a moment, then searched around the interior of the boat.

"Chris," he said, locating what he was looking for, "hand me that thing."

Chris walked to corner of the deck, picked up a long pole that was secured to the inner bulwark. Jim noticed a large, shining hook at one end.

Jack took the hook, handed Chris the flashlight.

"Jack, what are you doing?" Henry said, fighting for relevance to the situation.

"Take it easy, pop," Jack said casually. "Jim wants to

know if the Cap is really dead." Then, to Chris. "Hold it on the fat bastard."

Chris shone the light onto the writhing mass of barnacles that had been the captain.

Jack approached, slowly, warily, as if the things might leap from the captain onto his own exposed flesh. He held the long rod in front of him like a tribesman might hold a spear against a voracious tiger.

He stuck the top, rounded metal of the hook into the middle of the mass on the deck, right where the belly swelled up and down. With a flick, Jack twisted his wrists, then stabbed forward. He grunted as he felt the point of the hook dig in, snag on something meaty.

He pulled back with a quick tug of his elbows, and yelled a curse.

The captain split open like a punctured sack; the contents of him splashed furiously out onto the deck. Intestines mixed with wriggling creatures and hard black acorn-sized shells.

"Oh no," Henry whined, and now it was Chris backing up quickly, ramming his back against the wheelhouse.

"Oh shit!" Jack yelled, leaping away from the flow as it splashed toward him. Without thought, Jim hopped up onto the coaming, gripping the handrail above the shelter. He heard his father squeal and tuck his knees up onto the bench, then awkwardly tried to reach his feet, like the cartoon image of a fifties housewife jumping onto a chair at the sight of a mouse. Under different circumstances, it might have been comical.

"Dad, be careful!" Jack screamed.

The cushion beneath Henry's feet slid out from under him and he fell backwards, letting out a loud, whining shriek. His back crashed down against the edge of the boat, and Jim heard something snap, and his father flopped backwards, off the boat, and into the sea with a quiet splash.

"Dad!" Jim screamed, knowing it was too late.

"Fuck!" Jack yelled, running to the side of the boat, looking down into the dark water. Carefully, stepping around the massive lake of tubes and goo that was once the captain's insides, he went to the rear of the boat, looked behind them.

"Dad!" he yelled, flashing the light into the water. "Dad!" he screamed again, agony in his voice.

They waited a moment, then a moment more. Waiting for a cry for help, a splashing panic, a scream of terror as the things attached themselves to him. But there was nothing. Just the soft sound of the waves and the creaking of the dying boat. Jack dropped his chin to his chest.

Their father was gone.

JIM DIDN'T CRY, and Jack didn't know what to say. They watched the water for nearly an hour, waiting, calling. Jim was numb with the shock of seeing his father die. Now only the three of them remained, scared and desperate, very much alone.

"Guys, listen," Chris said, breaking the silence. "We gotta burn them."

They were sitting in the front of the boat, huddled against the dark, damp, cold night, the sea whispering sweet songs of death all around them.

"Burn them how, Chris?" Jack said, only the slightest tinge of mockery in his voice.

"Look," Chris continued excitedly, "we pour the fuel all around the perimeter of the boat, right? Then, we light it, burn all the bastards to crispy treats."

"And... what?" Jim snapped. "Just sit here on the boat and watch it burn around us?" Jim's usual fear of Chris was replaced by a depthless anger and sorrow for his father's death. They were all going to die out here, he knew that now. It was only a matter of time, and he'd be damned if he'd sit and listen to Chris's stupid-ass ideas while he waited for it. "That's retarded, Chris."

"Hey," Jack snapped, "don't use that word."

Jim gawped at his brother. "Oh, I'm sorry, Jack. I apologize for my insensitivity."

"Guys, just take it easy," Chris said.

For a moment, the very briefest of mad moments, Jim forgot about dying. He forgot about watching his father—who he loved and who had raised him alone, had done his best to care for him—fall away into the infested ocean right before his eyes. He forgot about his exhaustion, and sickness, and the horror of their situation.

For the briefest moment they were all kids again, sitting in the basement, playing video games, or dime poker. Mom was upstairs, cooking them lasagna, and Dad was on his way home from work. They'd watch a movie later, and the older guys would sneak liquor from the cabinet upstairs after the folks went to bed, but Jim would only have a sip because he hated the taste and the way it made him feel. The empty-headedness made him sick and scared.

But now those kids were here. Jack out of prison, Chris a foreman at his father's company. Jim freelancing as a software programmer, living in the same room he grew up in. His parents—both his parents now—dead. Gone.

A feeling of emptiness washed over him, cleaned him out. Now, out here in the dark, afraid and soon to die, he was a shell of who he thought he was. An empty vessel—fragile, dying and worthless. Even worse, he didn't know if he even cared what happened to him, to the others. In the dark night, floating on the great ocean, life seemed more passing. Their new world was death now, a dark place dominated by a split horizon of black water and a sooty, starless sky. He felt like a speck in this world, as insignificant as dust. There was no blanket of stars, no stunning cosmos in the heavens to pray to. The bowl of space hung blank and desolate and uncaring as the water.

They would all die soon, and his only hope was that his soul, or his energy, or whatever it was that lived on, if anything at all, would find something better than all this. Find something to love about life's miracle, which more and more seemed like the ultimate joke. They were but animate flesh on a planet as inconsequential as they were. They all tried so hard to live and to feel, desperate to understand the why of it all, time and time again, but they simply lived and died by the billions, and never, not once, did they feel truly alive, were no closer to answering the biggest questions, the ones that mattered. The imagination organ let humanity see God in their minds but still, somehow, the point was missed, leaving a planet full of idiots. For that failure the species was being punished. Wrathfully. The earth was taking the flesh back from beneath, retribution rising, released and hungry, wiggling and mighty and dark, to suck humanity down into the formless primordial stink of pre-existence. It was time for someone else to try and solve the riddle because Jim's turn, he knew, was just about over.

He heard his brother and Chris arguing, but he'd tuned them out, was listening to the soothing whispers and claps of the waves, the skittering, crackling sound of the crustaceans as they overtook the boat slowly, inch-by-inch, dragging it down into the sea. He almost smiled at the rush of peace that coursed through him, the knowledge that it would soon be over, that the end was so near...

"Oh my god!" Chris screamed, and stood so abruptly his hip shoved Jim into the side of the boat. He pointed, and both Jack and Jim, recovering, turned to look.

In the distance, from the direction Jim assumed must be the shore, was a light. A spotlight.

A boat.

No, not just a boat, Jim thought, his mind taking in the size and speed of the vessel, his dark thoughts shoved to the back of his mind, a rescue boat.

"I think that's the Coast Guard," Jack said, stunned, but Chris was already moving. He leapt up onto the rail, side-stepped his way toward the rear of the boat.

"Chris!" Jack yelled.

"The radio! We haven't been checking the radio, man!" Chris yelled back, already dropping down onto the deck and entering the wheelhouse. Jack and Jim stared through the glass as Chris grabbed the radio, began talking into it, saying, "Help," saying, "S.O.S."

Jack turned to Jim and smiled, slapped his back. "See, little brother, I told you I'd get you out of this."

Jim tried to smile, to find some comfort, but could not. He watched the boat, still so very far away. It was a small toy in the vast ocean, but it was getting closer, steadily closer.

"Yeah," he said, his eyes never leaving the oncoming beacon of light.

Jack hopped up onto the boat's bulwark, gripped the handrail and climbed up onto the top of the shelter, waving his arms like a lunatic, jumping up and down, finally gripping the large, blinking antennae and hollering like a coyote under the jolting white hemisphere of the distant moon.

It wasn't until Jack stopped screaming and jumping that Jim noticed Chris had disappeared. He looked through the glass, saw nothing but the darkened wheelhouse and a distorted sea beyond. He reached up, waved his hand, tagged his brother on the ankle.

"Jack!" he said.

Jack looked down, smiling like a winded teenager. "What?"

"Where's Chris?"

Jack looked at Jim, confused for a moment, then spun toward the rear of the boat. "Chris!" he screamed, and slid down from the roof, toward the deck.

Jim leapt up, followed Chris's path around the shelter, stopping near the rear, not wanting to leave the safety the height afforded.

The rear of the boat looked, to Jim, like a coral reef. Whatever had come out of the captain had somehow expanded, meeting up with the barnacles encroaching from the water to create a solid mass of black, writhing organisms. The air was putrid with the stench of brine and rot. Jim leaned forward over the lip of the roof, twisted and saw Chris, sitting on his ass on the floor of the wheelhouse, ripping the things off of his exposed ankles and calves.

"I don't know how, man, I don't know..." he was blubbering.

Jack had dropped down behind Chris, keeping Chris between him and the encroaching crustaceans. He carefully worked around his friend, plucking up the rubber suits that were not yet been covered by the things. He looked up and saw Jim watching.

"Take these," he said calmly. "Throw them up top there. Hurry, Jimmy."

Jim took the rubber suit pieces, one-by-one, and tossed them up onto the roof of the standing shelter, a space no more than six-feet by six-feet and dotted with antennas, a horn of some sort, and a box Jim assumed housed the emergency beacon.

After Jack handed him everything he jumped to the railing, waved one arm for balance, then climbed up onto the roof of the wheelhouse.

"Get up here," Jack said quietly, calm as could be.

Jim climbed up top, got on his hands and knees, turned to look at the boat's infested deck. He noticed, for the first time, that the rear of the boat was now dipping slightly into the water with each wave, white foamy sea slithering in, more and more, with every heave. It wouldn't be much longer, Jim knew, until the rear of the boat submerged, taking on the water from the hungry ocean by the hundreds of gallons, and all that swam within.

"Chris," Jack said, as if in eulogy.

Jim could hear Chris whining now, slapping at his legs ferociously, at his calves, his thighs. Jim bent forward, crouched low, looked down over the edge at his brother's best friend. He saw the white fleshy legs were nearly covered now, but still kicking. Chris was breathing fast and heavy, but he wasn't screaming, wasn't crying.

Then the legs disappeared, and he heard a gargled voice below say, "Fuck it." Jack looked down sharply as the scent of diesel fuel filled the air.

Jim heard the gurgling, could see it splashing onto the deck before Chris tossed the whole can toward the rear, where it continued to empty itself.

Furiously, Jack began grabbing pieces of the suit, wrapped one of the coats around him.

"Damn it, Jim, put the fucking suit on."

Jim got to his feet, and after a moment's hesitation, found the other pair of pants, pulled them on.

They were too big, and rubbery, and stank of mold. "What the hell are we doing, Jack?"

Jack was struggling with his own pants now, yanking them on one leg at a time. "We're gonna cover ourselves as best we can in this stuff, and then, and then we're gonna swim for it, little brother."

Jim stopped, panic scratching madly at the back of his brain.

"Swim?" he said, not able to keep the fear from his voice. "Did you see what those things did?"

"That's why we're gonna wear the suits, man," Jack said, and actually smiled at him. "It'll keep that shit off of us, okay? We just got to make it to that rescue ship, and it's close, right? Super close now, brother." He stood, fully wrapped in the yellow suit, and grabbed Jim's shoulders.

"Look, we'll stay here as long as we can. But if this thing starts to sink, we gotta jump for it and swim, okay? Otherwise we might get sucked down with it, and we won't be able to swim out."

"Oh man..." Jim whined, felt like crying. Jack helped him get the coat on.

"Here," he said, and began pulling strings, tightening everything as best he could, fussing with him like he was dressing Jim for the first day of school, or fixing his tuxedo jacket the night of the prom.

"My best man," Jim said, and started crying.

"What?" Jack said, tucking Jim's coat roughly into the waist of the pants, trying to seal everything as best he could.

"You would have been my best man, Jack," Jim said, smiling through tears. "That is, if I ever would have gotten married."

Jack stopped, looked at his brother, his eyes wet and scared. "Come on, who'd want an ex-convict as their best man?"

"I would!" Jim said, sounding to his own ears like a petulant child trying to convince the world he was right, damn it. That he could be right, just this one time.

"Okay, Jimmy," Jack said quietly, looking him over. "Okay."

He tucked in his own jacket, pulled the pants as tight as he could, then bent over and tried, miserably, to tuck the thick rubber into his thin crew socks. He tilted his head, looked up.

"Tuck it into your socks, bro, you got thicker ones than I do, it might stay."

Jim started to bend over to do just that, when he saw Chris emerge from beneath the roof of the shelter.

"Oh, good Christ," he said.

Chris was covered up to his belly in dark barnacles. They were spotted along his arms, his hands, the back of his neck.

"Oh no," Jack said, looking down at his friend.

Chris turned, looked up at the brothers, his height bringing the top of his head almost to their feet. His face swarming, misshapen. He opened his mouth to speak, and a few of the things slithering over his face slid quickly inside. He closed it, looked perplexed, then gagged, choked, swallowed.

As Jim watched, the jelly-like things on Chris's face turned color, stuck themselves to his flesh then, before his eyes, oozed black inky fluid through their translucent gel-like bodies, blacking and hardening in a matter of seconds.

Chris tried to open his mouth again, perhaps to scream, but instead he twisted, jerked, smashed his hands into his face, clawed at himself. Jim noticed he held a stick in his hand.

A flare.

Chris stepped backward, stumbling. He waved his arms, pushed through the infestation, away from the brothers. He brought his hands together, only a few fingers on each one still probing through the creatures rooted to him and sparked the fuse. Without hesitation, he lunged toward the rear of the deck, right into the heart of the swarming organisms.

"Jim!" Jack yelled, jumping from the roof of the shelter down to the deck at the head of the ship.

Jim watched one more moment, long enough to see the flare burst into red flame, to see Chris fall, the flare with him. He saw the fuel ignite over the swarm of creatures, spreading across the rear deck of the boat in a whoosh, covering it like a liquid yellow blanket.

Jim turned and jumped after his brother as the can erupted, blowing an explosion of broiling flame through the wheelhouse, blasting shards of glass outward into the night. As he dropped through space, he felt glass sting his leg, his arm. He saw Jack's face sliced into thin lines of red, his screams engulfed by the eruption.

Jim landed hard, collapsed to the deck, Jack fell on top of him, still screaming. "We gotta jump," Jack screamed, almost sobbing now. "We gotta swim, oh fuck..." he said, touching the mask of blood that was his face. His bulging eyes burned bright yellow, reflecting the flames that threatened to consume them both within a matter of seconds. "We gotta go NOW!"

With a roar, Jack stood, pulled Jim up with him, pushed him toward the edge of the boat, which was tilting upward at an angle, reaching higher as the rear of the boat flooded.

Jim could see the spotlight of the rescue vessel past the bright hot flames. He could feel the incredible heat on the side of his face, could hear the crisping of his eyebrows as it baked his skin. He had time to wonder if the heat was melting their rubber suits when he was shoved toward the water. He caught the rail, looked down, saw the thick crustaceans, the dark water below. He turned, panic blinding him.

"Jack, please no," he whimpered.

Jack's blood-streaked face grinned, his burning eyes leaping out of his skull like a demon incarnate. "Time to go, little brother!"

He leapt and rammed hard against Jim, who tried to push off with his feet in order to clear the things covering the sinking, burning vessel. In the split second before he impacted with the water, his brother wrapped around him in a bear hug, he heard Jack yell into his ear, "Keep your mouth closed!"

Then they hit.

The water slammed into him with an explosion of roaring, freezing cold, and Jim fought to keep his mouth shut, his eyes sealed. He could feel the heat behind him, the deafening roar of the boat cracking open, groaning in its final death throes.

Something hit him hard on the shoulder—Jack, kicking away—and it knocked his balance even more askew.

He opened his mouth to scream, realized a split-second too late what he was doing, and shut it while simultaneously blowing water out, back into the sea.

He swam away from the heat, away and up, breaking the surface with a gasp. He couldn't see anything, couldn't feel anything. He breathed in deeply, realizing with mad hope that his face felt clear, free of any parasites. He saw the spotlight approaching fast now, only a few hundred meters away. He could hear the loud engine, hear men screaming.

He swam toward it, his rubber-covered floppy arms fighting his advance, making it hard for him to get up any speed in the water. Massive waves, so much bigger than they seemed from the boat, lifted him, dropped him. The light of the oncoming ship would appear, disappear, then appear again. He turned, only for a second, saw Jack swimming like mad behind him.

Behind Jack was their boat. A ball of flame contrasting, like water in the desert, against the vast ocean surface. Something loud snapped, like a splitting two-by-four, and there came a soft bellowing, a detonation beneath the waves. Most of the boat had sunk into the water now, only the wheelhouse and madly waving antennae still visible when Jim spun himself around, continued swimming toward rescue.

"Keep going... Jimmy..." he heard Jack say from behind him. Jim wondered why the idiot wasn't keeping his mouth shut like he'd told him to do. "Keep going, brother!"

Jim did keep going. He swam, harder and harder, the thrill of knowing how close he was to safety, to living, energized him. He was going to make it.

He turned, smiling, wanting to wait for Jack, wanting to share this with him.

Jack was gone.

In the distance, the last flickers of the fishing boat vanished below the waves. The water surrounding Jim illuminated with a white incandescence as the spotlight of the rescue ship locked in on his position.

"Jack?" he said, then looked where the spotlight was filling the ocean.

They were everywhere. The water was filled with them. White, jelly-like creatures, shaped like tiny, gelatinous crabs, surrounded him. He was immersed in them.

The rescue boat killed its engines, rising up above Jim, two-stories high and built like a warship. A voice came booming from a loudspeaker, telling him to stay where he was, that they were sending help.

He saw a raft with an engine lower from a pulley, then release and hit the water, three dark shapes inside. The boat sputtered over the waves, racing toward him.

As he floated, he felt strangely buoyed by the creatures in the water. His flesh tingled, and his body felt eerily numb. He lifted his fingers, looked at them as if for the very first time. The crab-like creatures, no bigger than fat tadpoles, slid off his skin, back into the ocean. His mind buzzed, and the back of his neck tingled.

He could feel his muscles expand, and relax. There was the slightest pressure behind his eyes, a tickling on the inside of his nose, at the back of his throat. His tongue felt covered in jelly, and he suddenly wanted nothing more than to open his mouth and drink from the salty ocean water, drink it all down, fill himself with it.

Jim forgot about his brother, about his father, about his mother, about the boat. He felt... at peace.

Jim? Was it... Jim.

The boat reached him and strong hands pulled him up into the rubber raft.

"You okay, son?" one of the men yelled over the sound of the angry drone of the engine, speeding them back toward the ship. "Is there anyone else alive out here?"

Jim shook his head, could feel the probing at the back of his eyeballs, the rims of the sockets, the back of his lips. Something painlessly punctured his ear drum, slipped into his ear canal, then drew itself back.

Already a pressure was building in his abdomen, a growth. Swirling, dancing life. A new beginning.

A few moments later and they were strapping his body to a heavy harness, canvas and snapping locks securing him. He was lifted up into the air, dangling like dead weight, higher and higher, up toward the world of men.

The fathomless ocean crashed in great swelling heaves below him, on the deck above men ran and yelled as the heavy black sky watched impassively and the massive buzzing spotlight lit him up like a dripping wet savior being carried to heaven on the wings of angels. He closed his eyes and smiled as calm washed through him, every nerve-ending tingling, every part of him alive. He gloried in the power of the surrounding sea, and yet was eager for land.

# ABOUT THE AUTHOR

PHILIP FRACASSI, an award-winning author and screenwriter, lives in Los Angeles, California.

His stories have been printed in numerous magazines and anthologies, including *Best Horror of the Year, Dark Discoveries, Cemetery Dance, Lovecraft eZine, Strange Aeons* and others.

BEHOLD THE VOID, his debut collection of short horror fiction, has been translated into multiple languages, and was recently awarded "Short Story Collection of the Year" by *This Is Horror*.

He has published several standalone novellas, including *Shiloh, Fragile Dreams, Overnight* and *Sacculina*, which *The New York Times* praised as "...exciting, and terrifically scary."

Philip has been a professional screenwriter for over a decade and has several film projects in development. His produced films to date have been distributed by *Disney Entertainment* and *Lifetime Network*.

For more information on his books and screenplays, visit his website at www.pfracassi.com.

You can also follow Philip on Facebook, Instagram (pfracassi) and Twitter (@philipfracassi).

9 781590 217344